DAYS LIKE GRASS

MARK WARRINGTON

WestBow Press books may be ordered through booksellers or by contacting:

WestBow Press
A Division of Thomas Nelson & Zondervan
1663 Liberty Drive
Bloomington, IN 47403
www.westbowpress.com
844-714-3454

ISBN: 978-1-6642-8662-7 (sc)
ISBN: 978-1-6642-8661-0 (e)

Print information available on the last page.

WestBow Press rev. date: 3/20/2023

For Mom
Wish you could've read this.

CONTENTS

1

"THE FLOWER FADES"

(IS. 40:8)

The sun was shining. Its light touched everything, painting the world with its gilded sheen. Trees and shrubs shone brightly, grass was a brilliant green, including patches that were struggling, and even the squirrels and birds, with all their frittering, frittered in the beautiful glow of its rays. The sky was mostly clear, save for a lone cloud here or there that floated quietly by without imposing on anyone. A breeze was light but flowing and was most welcome to anyone working outside.

It was certainly being appreciated by Edy Baldy. Well, sort of. She would thank God for the wonderful breeze in between grumbling about the heat. Her complaint was unfounded, though. It was a normal, late summer day, for one. Secondly, nobody forced her to wait until 10 o'clock to start her outside work. Also, she was mostly shaded under a wavering old maple tree. She knew, however, that she'd be far worse off with no breeze at all and that she had been blessed. She thanked God again and continued working.

The object of her toil was a bed of lilies.—Day lilies, to be exact. Edy Baldy was working on her lilies. This was nothing out of the ordinary to anyone who knew her. To anyone who knew her it wasn't even worth mentioning; it was understood. It was late summer, the lilies were blooming beautifully, and the competition was in three weeks. Edy paused briefly to smile to herself before returning to work. "Competition" seemed a small word to her when talking about the Mureau Heights Garden Club End of the Summer Best Blooms Award. The gardening society was held in high esteem by its members. In Mureau Heights it was said you were either a member or you knew someone who was. Despite the adage, those who weren't in the Club didn't care about it, although it was often mentioned to out-of-towners. Edy was only a member because it was a requirement for entering the contest. Otherwise, she wasn't very invested. It was more about status. Not just for her, though. There was a certain snobbery to it that ignored the certificate and the five hundred dollar cash prize. Edy always felt the others were too snooty for her, but she never missed an opportunity to tell someone she was a member.

Aside from this, there wasn't anything particularly special about the town. It was one of hundreds of cities whose names were pronounced different ways, by visitors and residents alike. Edy always stood her ground that the correct pronunciation was Myur-ROW, but she often heard Muh-ROW, Murrow, MYUR-row, Muh-ROO, and even Marrow. There were whispers in the oldies community that their grandparents had spelled it Mereau, but nowhere in any town archive did this spelling appear. It did boast the highest number of mayors who had served in the military, and for a few years in near remembrance the town motto was "The Most Patriotic City in the Union." A kitschy little eatery called The Waffle Hut with architecture and décor to be envied was favored among many residents. The giant circular waffle atop the roof with the melting pat of butter which lit up at night drew as many patrons as the waffles did. Perhaps the gardening club deserved the central focus of the tourism committee.

Edy had been a member for about fifteen years but had only been competing for the last six. Always a gardener, she joined with hopes of learning how to improve the beauty of her plants before entering them. She quickly learned, however, how tight-lipped people in the club were, suspicious that someone might steal their secrets to defeat them in the contest. Undismayed by this, she pressed on.

Bless her heart, she had not yet won. It wasn't entirely her fault, though. Some of her losses could be contributed to inexperience, yes, but there had been storms, there had been pests, there had been disease. One year, a heatwave and a drought had formed an alliance to destroy almost everybody's flowers, leaving a winner practically by default, with a bouquet of dahlias that weren't very impressive. But this year…*this* year Edy was feeling good. She felt confident. She felt her experiences had taught her well. This was her year; she just knew it. The lilies were gorgeous, the weather was favorable, the bugs were off terrorizing someone else. This had to be her year. She wished she could check out the competition, but there was an odd phenomenon in Mureau Heights, wherein as soon as someone joined the gardening club a privacy fence shot up from the ground all around their yard. Edy took it positively, though. She saw it as an opportunity to focus on making her flowers the best they could be, the best she had ever grown, and not worry about what everyone else was doing. And they were the best she had ever grown. Still, she knew someone else could have prettier flowers. Mrs. Leslye was a three-time winner over the course of nine years and was always a favorite for a fourth. Mrs. Baker was last year's winner after having only moved to Mureau Heights the year before. Then there was Mr. Bucknut, who lived just down the street from Edy. He had pretty flowers…and the snobbish upturned nose of a monarch. He had never won either, but his finely groomed horseshoe hairstyle and pencil thin moustache sent Edy into a tizzy sometimes. Such is life, she knew. The haystack on top of her head probably made someone else feel the same way. The drama of it all was just so absurd at times, she had to periodically stop and humble herself. She quoted Isaiah.

"The grass withers, the flower fades," she took a deep breath, "but the word of our God stands forever."

She bent back down, grabbing another handful of eggshells. Edith Wilhelmina Baldy possessed very few qualities desired by the world, but her faith in God was rocksteady. She had been raised in a nominally Christian home but didn't truly accept Christ until her late twenties. She was hit hard with the conviction of her fallen state and need for a savior. Though she never considered herself an intellectual, it seemed to her the most logical thing in the world to submit to Christ and follow Him always. It was a deep faith with which she served her Lord, the kind of simple faith He Himself commended during His earthly ministry. It was the driving force in all her thinking. She wasn't exactly evangelical in that she didn't go out of her way to share the Gospel, but her ears were bigger than they looked whenever a moral issue was being discussed close by. Her theology was erroneous in some areas, but this was common of those who had been saved during the Jesus Movement of the 1970s. She could be seen as belligerent from time to time with her religious opinions, derided by some for standing her ground while praised by others for having immovable faith.

She was happy to have gardening as her source of exercise and fresh air. Easing slowly into her sixties, life moved a little slower than it once had. Having always been big boned, she had a normal physique for someone her age who had given birth twice. Poor eyesight had plagued her since she was a girl, and her corrective lenses got thicker and thicker every year. Arthritis rendered her handwriting almost illegible, which was unfortunate for friends and family as she did not embrace the technology of the 21st century. She had a computer, but no one knew why. Her oldest son, John, used it far more often than she did. She didn't mind, though. She was happier outside.

She was humming through a smile when a familiar sound broke into her tune. It was her telephone ringing; she could hear it through the open kitchen window, despite the birdsongs she found more appealing. She didn't stop working. Her husband and oldest son were both home, so one of them could get it. Focused as she was, after three rings her brow began to furrow. Surely one of them would get it before the machine picked up. Another ring, now she was annoyed. The fact that she had an answering machine was, for her, not an excuse to ignore a ringing telephone. A fifth ring, and she jerked her gardening gloves onto the ground and stood up to shuffle inside. Her machine was old and finnicky; sometimes if you picked up the phone after the recording started it would disconnect the call.

Barely making it inside before the beep, she was winded and irritated that she had to stop what she was doing outside while there were two people inside with spontaneous hearing impairment. Still, she managed the same old hello that those close to her knew so well. There was silence on the other end, and Edy asked again.

"Edith?"

It was her sister's voice, and only a sister would be able to perceive the distress in her single word.

"What is it, Caroline?"

Another pause.

"Dad died."

Edy's mouth hung open for the slightest pause before she blurted out,

"No he didn't."

2

"WHERE YOU GO"

(RUTH 1:16)

Edy was speechless. And stunned. Staring out the kitchen window, in the direction of her lilies but far beyond them, and at nothing really at all, Edith Baldy was speechless and stunned. She hung the towel back on the rack even though her hands were both still half wet. She had just gotten off the phone with her sister, who shouldered the burden of telling Edy their father had died. Now she was alone, but the kitchen didn't feel just empty—it was desolate. Desolate because there should've been someone there for her, but there wasn't. Harry and John were… wherever, and she was alone. The salmon color of the floor tiles she had specifically selected for their rose-pink hue now looked a sickly, pale red, and the yellow walls felt sticky even though she wasn't touching them. The cat clock that meowed the time at the top of every hour suddenly began to call from the back room.

Edy sat down at the table. Not for fear of falling, she

wasn't the type, but she was overwhelmed. It was a modest table, but fashionably so, as if to say she liked nice things but wasn't frivolous or gaudy. Her father was ninety-one and had lived in congestive heart failure for seven years, but the news of his death still struck Edy like a punch to the gut. She wasn't a blubbery person to begin with, but the circumstance, by nature, gave her the right to blubber. Yet there was no one around, and she didn't want to waste good blub. Still, despite the vivid emotionality of the moment, Edy did what she always did in moments where she felt swept over by ocean waves. She bowed her head.

"Father, I know You're with me."

As she opened her eyes she felt truly refreshed in spirit. Now she could go back through her conversation with Caroline. After Edy's disbelief came a puckered rebuttal from her sister that she had, in fact, not made it up. Her father had died peacefully in his sleep. Edy went in her mind to fond memories of her as a girl playing with him, but it was almost as though she had made herself do it, like she thought it was what she should do. Caroline brought her out of it, rather annoyed, and hurriedly informed her that she had to come home for the funeral and to handle all the affairs of the estate. Caroline ended the call with a lack of feeling and a coldness. Edy only perceived it now in her recap, but what could she do? The little girl in her memory wanted to stick her tongue out, but that would be ridiculous, she knew. Especially since Caroline was no longer on the phone.

Edy felt flustered as she began to think about going home. It wasn't any big deal, really; she went out to her father's house once a year to visit. But Edy was the oldest of seven children, and her relationship with them had always been strained, as far back as she could remember. In the back of her mind, she began to fear this was not going to be easy. It would most certainly be painful, for a number of reasons. Her father was dead, for a start; she was officially in mourning. It felt so strange for her to say inside her head. She was in mourning. It was like saying "my husband" for the first time after getting married. So foreign, it couldn't be in reference to her, but it was. Edith Wilhelmina Baldy was in mourning. For another thing, there were grievances to be aired. Old grievances that they had all danced around for decades, but which their homecoming just would not be able to avoid. It all stemmed from childhood and culminated in social status.

Edy began to think about all the preparations for the trip and the details and facing her siblings and seeing her father in a coffin and...what about her lilies, and Harry, and...and...

Edy stopped herself to pray again. This was all happening so fast, and there was so much to do and plan and brace for. She reminded herself of God's faithfulness and took a deep breath. She picked one problem to address first: who would go with her? As the question rolled around her mind searching for an answer, she realized it had never occurred to her to go alone. There were so many emotions, she was going to need comforting when dealing with them all. Her husband should have been the automatic choice, but he wasn't. Thinking she heard his chair creak, she rolled her eyes at the thought. Harry was a willowy old ghost, who was decrepit beyond his years. Medicated for different reasons, he was hardly the rock-solid support Edy was going to need.

Harold Sherman Baldy had been born to a failed carpet baron with a fondness for Civil War history, particularly that of General William Tecumseh Sherman. His first name would have been Sherman, but his mother, being a native of Atlanta, strongly objected. This, she revealed to Edy, was not because of any loyalty to Dixie, but because she simply hated the name. When Harold was seven years old, an uncle began calling him Harry, stating that Baldy was a rather unfortunate name and if he went by Harry, he would spite it. Unfortunately, in his early twenties, his genes kicked in and the nickname succumbed to the surname. This twisted irony would follow him in a parade of ridicule for most of his life. When Harry was seventeen, he enlisted in the navy with parental consent. He had done so for his father's approval, seeking to cheer him up after the loss of his business. This added weight to an already crushing blow when Harry received word a week into basic training that his father had died of a heart attack. He spent the whole of his tour in The Mediterranean Sea and was on the island of Malta when the Six Day War began. However, his most interesting story from this time was about a bar brawl that broke out between some Greeks and Turks. Harry rather enjoyed the navy, but did not reenlist, being coerced by a relative to come take care of his widowed mother.

Harry had always been fascinated with railroad culture. Why he hadn't chosen a career as a conductor no one knew. He had a cousin in the business who was more than happy to get him in. Edy always thought it was more of a fantasy than a passion and that he wouldn't have enjoyed actually working in it, getting all too familiar with the everyday frustrations that one didn't see in the brochures. He had instead driven a dump truck hauling limestone for thirty years, hating almost every minute of it, despite the fact that it provided a modest life for his wife and two sons. His body steadily endured the normal wear and tear of the job, but Harry's career came to a sudden end when he fell from his truck and broke his hip. Physically, he made a near full recovery, walking away with only a slight limp, but mentally, something changed inside him. It was as though the incident jerked him out of a delusion that he would live forever, and he was faced with his own mortality. He was no spring chicken when it happened, yet his doctor said he was too young for the replacement surgery Harry inquired about. Everyone who knew him said the man who left the hospital was not the same one who'd entered it. A time warp was said to have occurred, as he was twenty years older when he went on disability. Ever after, he was frail and subject to the tyranny of a stiff breeze. Always cold, always sleeping, slow-moving (on the rare occasion that he did move), poor eating, he was a living memory of a man who was no more. And for some reason, his wife was fully devoted to coddling him in the years since his accident.

Harry was not a Christ follower. This was the true mystery within the family; no one could understand why. He had been raised in a nominally Christian home in a time when *nominally* Christian was the standard, and he was known as a spiritual person by those closest to him. He never gave an answer for his particular disbelief in God, but it was hard to accept it as just plain old hardheartedness and a refusal to be told what to do. If pressed on the subject, he would typically just blow up and yell about off-topic things that made him mad. He had a temper to match his father's, but he was never a violent man. Still, his anger was a defining trait in the memory of his sons.

Edy's next consideration was her oldest son, John. John Moses Baldy. Ever since she got saved, Edy loved the names Moses and Aaron and hoped she would have two sons to give them to. The trick, of course, was going to be convincing her husband to agree, what with his resistance to anything biblical. She cleverly earmarked them as middle names. The Lord graciously fulfilled her desire, and Edy told her husband he could nickname the boy Moe after his favorite Stooge. Harry went along with it, but the plan almost backfired when John was four. Seeking the affection of his father, he demanded his parents call him by his middle name. Edy wisely consented to calling him Moses, and *only* Moses. The child's resolution quickly died out, and John remained permanently.

A thrill seeker from early on, John entered the world of skydiving in young adulthood, much to the horror of his mother, who was of the "if God intended man to fly" school of thought. Harry had been indifferent about it but took an assuming approach to John's intent to go pro. John fully intended to do just that and was well on his way, but, sadly, in his early twenties he had an accident and broke his leg. The injury healed, but he felt slighted. When asked, he would say he was following doctor's orders. His doctor did say to forget about skydiving for a year, but afterwards, John being young and healthy, he could have at it if he wanted. Deep down, John knew why he had really quit. Vowing to never return to the sport, he locked up all his gear in a trunk, a tomb for the future that might have been. Now in his late thirties, having never moved out, he loitered around his parents' house, anti-social and lurky like a spider. He loved talking about music, so he worked part time at a record store telling people what they should listen to.

John was a Bible reader at a young age, largely due to Edy's insistence upon it and church attendance. He was proud of Christ and very outspoken about his faith, despite the social cost during his teen years. After his accident, though, his faith featured less and less in his speech. His mother, who could be naïve at times, never made the connection. Anymore, John was defensive when asked about his Christian walk.

Edy thought it would be good for him to go. It would get him out of the house. Plus, he could see his aunts and uncles, whom he hadn't visited in years. She picked up the phone to call him. He was one floor up, right above her head, no doubt, but Edy didn't want to have to climb the stairs to go to him, and he hated when she yelled up the stairwell. He answered flatly 'no,' as though turning down meatloaf for dinner, without any condolences for her mother's loss, and Edy thought nothing of it.

She hesitated for a moment before calling her other son, Geoffrey. It was only after Geoffrey Aaron's birth certificate was signed that Edy realized that Scripture's Aaron was actually older than Moses. By that point, she decided switching them would just confuse the children. Geoffrey had been for many years a black sheep in the family. Thus, it was a surprise to everyone when he joined the ministry in his late twenties, since he had lived, as he put it, "a less discerning lifestyle" prior to going to seminary. Geoffrey was left-handed, which wasn't particularly interesting, but as he was the only southpaw either of his parents were related to, Edy often mentioned it when discussing him with someone new. "I used to tell him he was adopted," she'd say and then laugh.

Edy was often hesitant before calling Geoffrey. She thought about texting him, but of course it was a terrible idea. She almost chuckled at texting *Grandpa's dead, need you to fly with me for the funeral.* It wasn't because he was married, and it wasn't because he was often busy with work or home. It was because he was so standoffish on the phone. She would converse, and he would just hover on the other end, speechless. Texting wasn't much better, though. She would text him something, sit, and wait. And wait. And wait. And finally, he would respond.

The truth was that Geoffrey loved his mother and tried to honor her biblically. He helped her often with different things around her house when he wasn't tied up. Still, she *was* his mother. She would call him with something usually mundane, ask him a question, and then never allow him the chance to spend the breath he inhaled for an answer before saying something else. She tended to digress so quickly and so deeply that he wondered seriously sometimes if she understood him picking up the phone as an invitation to tell her life story. Over the years, Geoffrey had come to view her calls as changing lanes in rush hour traffic. He had to look for the slightest opening and then leap in if he ever wanted to make it back home. Texting wasn't much better, though. He would read her texts when they came through, but almost always judging them not urgent, he would let them simmer awhile.—And occasionally, forget to respond.

When he wasn't spending time with his wife or dodging

his mother's communications, he was an associate pastor of Mureau Heights First Church-Baptist. Edy was ecstatic over his career choice, but not enough to join his flock. She was a longtime member of First Baptist Church of Mureau Heights and wasn't easily given to change. The flip phone in her hand was sure evidence of that. Still, she supported his church financially, though she did not mention this to anyone from her church. She was old-fashioned and had an odd sense of loyalty. He knew it wasn't personal, but Geoffrey couldn't help but be a little hurt. If nothing else, he wanted her to hear him preach. He was known to say that without her he may never have come to know Christ. She dialed the number.

"Hello, Mom."

He seemed to be in an agreeable mood, she thought as she told him the news.

"Oh, Mom, I'm so sorry," was his immediate reply.

For no particular reason, Geoffrey was never very close with his maternal grandfather. Neither one had reached out on a regular basis during Geoffrey's childhood. There was also a great geographical distance between them. So, at least subconsciously, he viewed this more as his mother's loss than his own. Nevertheless, his sympathy was genuine. Edy asked him about flying with her, and as she did, she thought how wonderful it would be to have a pastor with her. Surely, he would be the perfect grieving companion, always having the right thing to say, carrying his Bible around cradled in his arm like a football. She could share him with other people at the funeral who needed comforting. But what about the funeral officiant? Would it be rude to have a second pastor there? Would he see Geoffrey as an intruder? *Then it'd be awkward between them*, Edy thought, *and everyone would blame me for bringing him.*

"I really wish I could, Mom," Geoffrey interrupted her fretting, "but I'm sort of stuck here this week."

Edy's relief didn't last long enough to bite off her response.

"What do you mean, 'stuck'?"

"The church is getting new carpet this week and I have to oversee the job."

"Oh, shouldn't Glenn be doing that? At my church, the senior pastor always supervises those kinds of things."

Edy's brow would furrow when saying something passive aggressive. Luckily, she couldn't see his eye roll.

"Glenn's in Sarasota at a Business as Mission conference. Besides, I have a funeral on Sunday after service."

"Who died?"

Edy had a knack for tacky sidetracking.

"Stan Keurick."

"The deli man?"

"Yes."

Some lazy surprise, and Edy said, "I never liked his store. Sticky floors."

"Why can't Dad or John go with you?" Geoffrey got annoyed when he had to wrangle the cattle of her thoughts.

Geoffrey already knew why his father wouldn't be the best travel buddy. His brother, on the other hand...well, he wouldn't be ideal either, but at least he wouldn't have anything pressing keeping him from being there for their mother. Once very close, the two brothers rarely saw each other anymore. The relationship shifted after John's accident, which wasn't exclusive to Geoffrey. It worsened, however, when Geoffrey joined the pastorate, leading the younger to suspect the older of losing his faith, or at least turning his back on a holy God who had spared his life. Geoffrey also couldn't help but be annoyed when he was asked to do things his brother was completely capable of doing.

When Edy had finished defending her firstborn's excuses, Geoffrey spoke with her for a few more minutes and then had to go. Edy put the phone down. Loneliness began to close in on her and she thought she was going to cry. It wasn't the pain of losing her father, she knew; that hadn't sunk in yet. *Why do I feel so guilty about crying?* She was starting to dread the upcoming trip, as though if she had someone to go with her it would be a vacation of sorts instead of an uncomfortable family gathering that was sure to be dramatic and ugly. Edy looked at the woodcraft sign above the cookie jar, her mind seeking a distraction. HE WILL NEVER LEAVE YOU NOR FORSAKE YOU. The words of Moses were comforting. Edy loved that sign, with its purple lacquer and calligraphic text. It had been a birthday present one year from her best friend, Ruth. Just like that, Edy could almost reach up and touch the lightbulb above her head. She knew exactly who she could call.

As she dialed the number, Edy felt almost giddy that she had remembered Ruth. There was really no reason for her excitement, though. She saw Ruth all the time, but she knew in the instant that she thought of her that she would be the ideal moral support. Edy's devotion to protocol could sometimes fog her thinking. Perhaps asking her sons was just a way to tell them their grandfather had died without getting emotional. Suddenly it did feel like a vacation. *Best not to get excited too soon* she thought. Maybe Ruth wouldn't be able to go either.

When Ruth answered after three rings, Edy opened her smiling mouth wide, her eyes beaming brightly, and in a very cheery voice, she responded, "Hi."

And in the instant, her face dropped as she remembered what she was calling about.

"My dad died."

All the life was gone from her voice, and there was silence.

"Edy?"

"My dad died," she repeated, even flatter than the first time.

"Oh, honey, I'm so sorry. I'm coming over now."

Finally, Edy started crying. Not blubbering, just modest crying, but in Ruth she found permission to feel the pain of her loss. Her friend consoled her and made sure she was calm.

"Can I bring you anything?"

"Yes," Edy answered shakily. "Maybe some huckleberry ice cream."

"Edy, no one around here has that."

"Nature Foods does."

"That's in Templeton, honey. Half hour away."

"I'll pay your gas."

"No, sweetie, I mean it's ice cream. It'll be soup by the time you get it."

"Oh, right," Edy said. "Don't worry about it, then."

"I'm leaving right now. I'll be there in ten minutes."

Edy put down the phone and thanked God for Ruth. She couldn't stop her mind from worrying again about all that had to be done and taken care of, but she took a deep breath and waited patiently for her friend.

Ruth Krein had been Edy's best friend for over thirty years. They met through a mutual friend at a party and had been close ever since. For all they had in common there were some sterling differences. Whereas Edy wore her old-ladiness like a loud shirt, Ruth was just a woman who was getting on in years. She was mild-mannered and gentle, patient, and easy going, but never afraid to confront a wrong. She had experience in the world but was well disciplined. Despite the suppositions of many, she was in fact a Christ follower. She focused more on what the Lord did than what He said. Not that she thought little of His words; she just felt it was important to *show* people right living, and that it was too easy, when sharing Christ's words, to sound judgy and condescending. As such, she didn't often quote Scripture, but understood the morals very well.

She came from a large family, and immediately she was the third of five children. Ruth was no stranger to death. Many of her relatives, including two of her own siblings had passed already. Ruth had never married and was the only one of her siblings not to do so. She had simply never met a man she wanted to be old with, even though she lived as though she had no intention of ever getting old. She was energetic for her age and very self-reliant, rarely calling repairmen. She found a reason to get out of the house every day, even if it was just to take a walk.

When she arrived at Edy's house, Ruth found her friend right where she imagined she would: out back with her lilies. But Edy was clearly not paying attention to her flowers. She had most likely come out to admire them and take her mind off things but couldn't. Ruth announced herself and the two hugged for a long moment while Edy cried. They moved into the kitchen where Ruth made tea and set the box of doughnuts she brought with her on the table in front of Edy. Of course it was from her favorite shop on Main Street. She knowingly grabbed an old fashioned and bit into it. She admitted it did make her feel better.

Over tea, Edy told her friend what details she knew and about her desperate need to leave as soon as possible to be with her siblings.

"Who's going with you?"

Ruth's question was why Edy felt so blessed with her. She just understood.

"Well, actually," Edy was a little bit coy, "I was hoping you might."

Ruth rubbed her chin as she began to think out loud. Her face said that even if she couldn't go, she wanted to, and Edy saw it. Ruth had retired early but kept a job at a spice shop in the single block historic district of Mureau Heights. It was owned by a friend of hers and she usually only came in one day a week, just to stay busy. She occasionally had out of town family stay with her for a visit. But this was not one of those weeks, and she knew the shop wouldn't fold if she couldn't cover her shift. So, she happily agreed to go with Edy.

"But," she said with a finger, "we'll have to drive."

It was in that exact moment that Edy remembered Ruth's fear of flying, or rather, her fear of airplanes. As tough as she was, it wasn't being in the air that scared her. She had simply seen too many news reports of plane crashes and didn't want to end her life in one. Edy's mind started scrambling to put out all the fires. She knew the funeral hadn't been scheduled yet, but her siblings would still be annoyed at her. Flying would take about three hours; driving would take three days. Edy liked the idea, though. She felt a nice road trip with a good friend could help her ease into sibling mode.

Ruth couldn't help herself. She asked why John wasn't going. Edy defended him as she always did, and Ruth kept her eyes from rolling. She loved Edy, but the way she laid down for her oldest made her want to scream sometimes. She knew as well as anyone else why Harry wouldn't be going. She asked about Geoffrey, but her wording and tone were different.

"Will Geoffrey be attending the funeral?"

Ruth liked Geoffrey. She had an awareness that his mother didn't of all that he did for her, on top of everything else he had going on.

The two friends discussed the trip for a while, and then Ruth decided that if she was leaving for cross country in the morning she had better go home and get packing. Edy said that between driving and legal affairs and sibling affairs, it could be as much as two weeks. Ruth shrugged it off, happy to help. Just then, Edy's cat, Duke Archibald, came strutting into the room, seeking attention without wanting to be touched and demanding food without pity. Ruth was a dog person and didn't much care for cats.—Specifically, Edy's cat. She called him Sir Scratch because of his tell-tale hatred for Edy's furniture, or, if Edy was being particularly servile, Ruth would refer to him, in her best British accent, as "Duke, the arch-Baldy," which really irked her friend. Edy always said it was because of her cat allergy that Ruth treated him so, but Ruth just denied it. Edy bent down to pet him and jumped to a realization.

"Oh, my goodness! Who's going to feed you while I'm away?"

"How about your son," Ruth suggested, furrowing her brow.

Edy, ignoring Ruth's obvious tone, said, "Ooh, that's a great idea. Let me call Geoffrey real quick."

Ruth's eyebrows shot up above her head in disbelief. "Don't you dare call him for this. Make John do it. Shoot, even Harry could do that."

"No, no. I don't want him to fall bending over to pick up the bowl."

Edy already had her phone up to her ear, and Ruth jumped up from the table.

"I'll see you in the morning, dear."

As the disgruntled woman left, Edy waved her half goodbye, half be quiet. Just as the door closed, Edy started talking.

"Hello, Geoffrey? Listen…"

3

"SET"

(DEUT. 1:7)

Everything was coming together. Geoffrey had agreed to feed Duke Archibald. There wasn't any doubt that he would; he had taken after his mother's love of cats. Since he felt bad about not being able to go with her, it was the least he could do, but would he feel the same way when he discovered the rigid instructions for also tending the lilies? If he thought Duke's regimen was something… Edy didn't have time to pack for her trip and write the great novel of horticultural maintenance that Geoffrey would need to keep her garden in the running for first prize. The contest was just on the other side of this voyage, and her flowers were beautiful, but keeping them that way was going to require some very particular care. *He can handle it,* she thought to herself. *He's a smart boy.*

Ruth was also on board. Edy reflected on what a true friend Ruth was and what a blessing that she was available to just pick up and go with her. Truly amazing since Ruth was far from bone idle. Edy knew that it was all under God's omniscience, a winnowing of sorts, a divine process of elimination—like Gideon's army. She could relate to Ruth on so many levels, while also having the freedom of openness that blood could sometimes hinder. It went both ways, though. Edy had often offered the same comfort to Ruth. Being the middle kid in a family of five, Ruth had been the rope in the tug of war many times. It was a large family, whose bond was strong, but the tensions, at times, felt stronger.

Cat fed, lilies tended, friend secured. So why was Edy feeling so despondent and anxious? She was closer to some of her siblings than others, but she felt a bit of an outsider with all of them. Plus, it had been years since they had all been together in the same room, and now, to meet again under these circumstances, it was a volatile situation. What if she got into a fight with one or all of them? That wouldn't be very Christlike. What if there was road trouble? What if something happened at home while she was away? What if Harry hurt himself or got sick? What if something happened to her lilies? What if there was a tornado?

"Oh, really, Edith," she had to growl at herself. "Get a hold of yourself."

She remembered Isaiah 26:4. *Trust in the Lord forever. For in God the Lord, we have an everlasting Rock.* In moments like this, after recalling Scripture, Edy always released a deep breath she didn't realize she was holding. It made her feel better. She knew sitting in the kitchen chair hunched over wasn't helping anything, certainly not her posture, so she stood up and headed to the family room to tell Harry about her father. *He might as well know why I'm going to be gone for a while.* Then she knew she would head upstairs and start packing, most likely falling asleep before finishing.

The next morning, Edy woke around five, angry with herself for not finishing her packing. She had a few hours before she was supposed to pick up Ruth, but the very idea of falling asleep when there was work to do. *Really, Edith,* she thought hazily, *you're no better than Peter, James, and John in the garden.* She slowly made her way downstairs to make a cup of coffee, which, of course, she would sip outside while looking at her lilies. The sky was clear, and light was breaking in the east. It would be a sunny day, which made her smile. Looking at her lilies was often worrying about her lilies, but she did enjoy them, too. Staring at them now, she reflected on what lilies meant to her. Edy's mother, Nora, always kept such beautiful flowers. Nora Alice Finney was born exactly nine months to the day after her Irish parents stepped off the boat in America, leading to much snickering as to how they celebrated their arrival. Her father opened a flower shop after a few other jobs hadn't panned out, and it was moderately successful. Nora always told Edy that she had learned the secret to perfect daylilies from him. She died in childbirth when Edy was seventeen, before passing on this fabled secret, but Edy said it was in her blood and even told people her heritage would help her win the contest. Some day. So many years had passed since her mother died, but just then, remembering her face in the sunlight, smiling at her, Edy felt that pain again. *And now Dad's gone, too. I guess this is how it happens.* Edy realized time had truly marched on. With the steam gone from her cup and more packing to do, Edy went back inside.

She felt refreshed from the coffee, which was an odd

reaction, but she was calm. She looked at the heap of clothes on the bed and decided she was not the queen of England. Grabbing them to put them all back, she paused. *Well, I don't want to look like a bag lady, either.* She knew she could not show up looking like…well, the heap of clothes. She let them back down but resolved to quickly pick a couple of smart outfits, one funeral-appropriate outfit, and then some casual attire for in the car. Of course, there were climate changes to consider when covering so many miles. Two light jackets later…and some sandals. Sandals made her feet hurt if she wore them for more than an hour, but she had to have them. Which shoes for the funeral? She needed an umbrella—two umbrellas, actually. If it rained at the funeral, she had her fancy black umbrella that Caroline had brought her from Italy. It had been in public three times in twenty years. Edy knew it must've been expensive, so it was absolutely not an everyday umbrella. For informal, non-funeral, commoner rainy days, the five-dollar blue umbrella was better suited. *Edy, you said you were going to be quick.* Why was she so rushed? She knew her siblings would be irritated if she took too long in arriving. She finished packing, reminding herself that anything she forgot could be purchased practically anywhere.

"You're not going to the moon, Edith," she said out loud.

Only three pieces of luggage. Edy thought that was a personal best and turned to go downstairs but stopped abruptly. She knew she'd forgotten something. She couldn't carry everything in one trip, she knew, but she couldn't leave the room until…*ah, yes,* looking at the nightstand she reached out and grabbed her Bible. Now she could go. And then come right back.

Seven thirty. It was a good thing Ruth lived so close. The car was packed, the cat was fed, the lilies weren't due for a watering until tomorrow, so she was good there. She worked on a second cup of coffee as she illegibly wrote instructions for her second born to hold down the fort. Harry and John were both still asleep as the morning sun filled the house. Throwing all the curtains open was Edy's passive aggressive alarm clock. Her eyes scanned the room, and her mind scanned the checklist. Everything was covered. It was time to go.

She pulled into Ruth's driveway just a few minutes before eight, already smiling. Happy that she was early and feeling the crispness that comes from setting out on a trip in the early morning. So many people still asleep or not yet dressed for the day, and Edy was wide-eyed with two hands on the wheel already. She looked at Ruth's flowers. Beautiful asters that had just bloomed stole the show in her landscaping, but Ruth was always more fond of her big rose of Sharon with its pinkish-red flowers. It always amazed Edy that this skilled gardener didn't compete with her and the rest of the club. Ruth was a competitor for years, and then one year she volunteered to judge. She felt the winner that year had been chosen very underhandedly, and she quit the club flat out. She didn't like to talk about it much, but she did always claim that her flowers had always done better after her departure because now she just gardened because she loved it, not to win a prize. Edy had to admit her display did have a relaxed look to it, a quiet humility that didn't boast its expertise. Ruth came out of her front door and set her one suitcase down so she could lock up. She was wearing shorts and a button up short sleeve shirt, which was typical of her, yet she always looked nice. She went to the back of the car as Edy popped the trunk, and took notice of all the luggage. As she got into the car, Edy smiled warmly.

"Good morning."

Ruth's smile was naturally kind, even as she said, "So many clothes, did you finally move out of that madhouse?" Then both ladies laughed as Edy backed out of the driveway. The sun beamed blindingly bright as an early morning summer sun does. It was going to be a beautiful day. Approaching the interstate, Edy saw the sign that read "Now leaving Mureau Heights," and for the first time she pondered it, taking note that it did not invite the reader to return.

Edy didn't acknowledge it, but her mood changed almost immediately as they got on the interstate and left Mureau behind them. The sky was a cool blue, with scattered clouds that didn't interfere with the sunlight. It was so much bigger out in the open, without all the trees and buildings boxing her in. With so much anticipated awkwardness ahead, it was strange that she would breathe in the taste of freedom while leaving home. Still, it was undeniable she seemed happier. Ruth always noticed when Edy felt unencumbered. It happened so seldomly, a close friend like Ruth could hardly miss it. The two women were perfect traveling companions; they liked a lot of the same music, the oldies they were called now. Ruth was very keen and knew her friend was a knot of emotions inside. She wanted her to enjoy herself in moments like these and not be weighed down, but she also didn't want Edy to ignore the reality of the situation. It would take craft and skill to guide her through this ordeal. She needed to get Edy talking. It didn't matter what about, she just needed to spend the oxygen. Ruth knew it would all come out. Besides, they had three days before they reached their destination. There was lots of time to unload.

"So, what's Caroline been up to?" she began.

Edy took the bait as though with an unconscious 'I thought you'd never ask' approach. She began telling Ruth about her sister's trip to The Bahamas in the spring. Ruth knew it wouldn't have made any difference how she started the conversation, a history of the subject would always ensue. She could never remember how the woman jumped from any random question to something they did a decade ago, but she certainly had a talent for it. And as far as Ruth was concerned, they had been friends for a great many years, and no doubt, Ruth had heard all of it before, but—as long as Edy wasn't sitting silent behind the wheel.

Caroline Francis was the third of the Wimmer children. Surprisingly, growing up, her strongest tie to her only sister was gender. Despite a degree in hospital administration, she got her realtor's license in her mid-twenties and married Horace Langley, a corporate taxman who did very well for himself. Caroline was no slouch, though, in her profession, but after Horace's promotion to senior executive ten years ago she hadn't sold a house since. She often teased the idea of "returning to work," but she knew as well as anybody there was no reason at all for her to actually do so. She lived in a wealthy neighborhood, just her and her husband, and their dog, Terry, a Norwich terrier. Her guilty pleasure was professional hockey. It stood in stark contrast to every other facet of her life, but she was a fanatic and could become quite rambunctious at the games.

As Edy warmed up to the subject at hand, Caroline

was endeared anew to her heart. She remembered wishing at the time her sister was born that her parents would have stopped, that their brother, Thomas, would be trapped forever between to inseparable sisters. This was beyond her control, of course, and the Lord in His wisdom saw fit to show her just how far.

Of course, just mentioning Thomas then shifted her train of thought. Thomas Randall was born two years after Edy. Often considered the black sheep of the family, instead of college he chose a trade school and became a union electrician, a career that was far more lucrative than people thought. He married his first wife at twenty-six, and they divorced after two years. His second marriage came four years later and had lasted ever since. Ironically, Edy liked his first wife better. Thomas was a fish lover. Not a fisherman, though. He was always quick to explain the difference between the two lifestyles. Edy's husband had some difficulty understanding this when they first met. Somewhat of a fisherman, he thought it would be easy to bond with Thomas over some worms and silence in his canoe. Thomas, however, wasn't interested in the capturing (and certainly not the eating) aspect of fish. He was fascinated by fish culture and enchanted by the colors. Without children, he could easily afford the very expensive hobby, which he said was far more than a hobby. He had many fish tanks in his large house, with different lighting arrangements to cater to the fish inside. Occasionally, someone would ask him how much his fish were worth, and he would always answer 'enough to have their own insurance policy.'

Ruth kept her eyes and her mind moving as Edy continued to talk. She was happy her friend was unwinding, but she could sometimes become distracted by conversation, and Ruth didn't want her to detour two states over before realizing they had missed an exit. She had directions pulled up on her phone, and, like a good navigator, was checking them regularly. She had been mostly silent thus far, and gladly listened to Edy tell her story.

Andrew Martin came after Caroline. Through a college friend, he went to work for a major tire company in their marketing department a week after receiving his diploma. He began with automotive tires, then moved on to big truck tires, then farm implements, before finally focusing on racing tires. Nicknamed 'King Midas,' he doubled the profits of every product he worked with within the first year, which led to a great many raises and promotions. He was obsessed with his personal appearance, especially his hair, which, at fifty-five, should not have been as jet black as it was. He married a woman as shallow as he was, and they both agreed they were too busy and just plain disinterested to raise children. When he was transferred to France for a year, he got a taste for travel and he and his wife made globetrotting their lifestyle.

Wesley Noel was next. He was the only one of the Wimmer brood to not move out of state, and always claimed to be closest to their father. He was a highly successful architect who had opened his own firm several years back. He had also been married three times. Divorce, annulment, divorce, he said he was always up for another try. People joked that he was never with anyone long enough to have children, and, now in his early fifties, he considered that particular ship sailed. His pastime was medieval woodworking, which was considered strange by almost everyone. His siblings dished out their fair share of ridicule for it, except of course, his oldest sister. Edy had always admired not just his skill but his devotion, passion, and flair for historical accuracy. For this, he had gifted her a cedar chest one year for Christmas, which she cherished and bragged about and used to this day at the foot of her bed.

Stuart James followed older brother Wesley three years later. His closest sibling relationship was with sister Caroline for no particular reason. Their personalities were just very alike, and they were always chummy. It was because of this that Stuart took after Caroline in the realty game, surpassing her own degree of success even before her indefinite hiatus. Stuart was married, without children, to a woman that no one saw any chemistry with, yet they had remained wedded for twenty years. Stuart was a cinema buff.—Not a movie buff, as many often tried to correct. His great passion was black and white films from the thirties and forties. For many years, he even wore slicked back hair and a pencil thin moustache to emulate the great John Barrymore.

The last sibling, the baby of the bunch, was Henry Ford Wimmer. Henry was the superstar of the whole family. For one thing, he was still in his forties; just when his parents thought that six was enough, along came Henry seven years after Stuart. Henry was also a heart surgeon, one of the top ten in the country to be exact. His brothers and sister, Caroline, were all very well to do, yet they made it clear they envied Henry's money. He acted somewhat snobby toward them, but with Edy he was different. Not kind or friendly per se; he saw her as more of a parental figure. There were seventeen years between them, and she had indeed been forced to mother him for much of his childhood, her young adulthood. On the rare occasion that he saw Edy, he always showed her the high life that she couldn't afford. Not so much to spoil her as to show her he had made it, something many children seek to show their parents. It was more than just approval. It was almost as though he wanted her to know he was okay, to soothe the anxiety of a worrisome mother. Henry never married and was hailed an ever-bachelor. He always said he was leery of gold diggers, but the real truth that he never voiced aloud was that he had no faith in marriage. His siblings, with the exception of Edy, had shown him divorce, superficial status marriages, and joyless marriages that his romantic side wanted nothing to do with. He admitted that he desired love but had no interest in walking down the aisle. He was an avid lover of boats and the sea. He, too, had made the mistake long ago of inviting Thomas to fish off his yacht.

Edy admitted that she never wanted brothers when she was younger. When Thomas was born, she reasoned that it was only fair to have one of each. Then Caroline came, and Edy planned to team up with her sister and torment their brother. Andrew balanced the scales, and Edy figured it would be a fair fight. Then three more boys.

Edy looked at a billboard, gave a deep sigh, and reloaded her lungs. She began to untangle the web of years for the benefit of Ruth, who had indeed heard all of these things over the years. She sat and listened to Edy, believing that, though she was familiar with the facts, she knew there were things that Edy had always kept locked away. Feelings, opinions, thoughts, arguments, Edy was not very confrontational with her family, and Ruth thought the present circumstances might draw some things out of the vault, as though if she heard herself telling the same stories over and over, eventually she would hear how ridiculous it all was. She was mostly interested in Edy being honest with herself, but some part of her wanted the dish. Ruth's own family was no model of perfection, so she understood drama, but it angered her how Edy was always laying down for people who should be more respectful of her. Blunt without being coarse, she never shied from telling Edy how she felt.

Suddenly, a muffled kaboom disturbed their thoughts as the car began to shake. Edy was panicked, and Ruth quickly assured her it was a blowout. Edy pulled the car to the shoulder and put it in park. She asked Ruth for the motor assist directory in the glove box, and with an *are you serious?* expression she told Edy to pop the trunk. Edy nervously objected as though Ruth changing the tire would undo the fabric of society.

"And put your blinkers on," Ruth added, stepping out of the car.

Edy complied in a flush, knowing she wouldn't stop Ruth. She quickly prayed, asking God to protect Ruth on the side of the highway, thanking Him for safely guiding them to the shoulder. She thanked Him for Ruth and asked for blessing on her knowledge and skill. When she opened her eyes, she suddenly realized the sky was grey. *When did we lose the sun?* she wondered, as she jumped out the car, almost getting the door ripped off by a passing car she had failed to check for. She feared Ruth wouldn't be considerate to everything in the trunk, in light of the task at hand. Carefully moving things onto the ground, which she complained about doing because she didn't want them dirty, Edy cleared the way to get the tire and jack out. Ruth got to work.

Looking back to the sky, Edy immediately worried about her flowers. *What if it rains? They're not due for water today, and it's a little late in the day for water anyway.* She would have to check in with Geoffrey when they got to their hotel and find out if it rained back home, because if it did, she would have to tell him to not water tomorrow morning.

When Ruth was finished changing the tire, Edy anxiously supervised putting the flat tire in the hole in the trunk. She started grabbing luggage, and Ruth stopped her.

"I would put that in the back seat if I were you."

"Why?" Edy asked, completely oblivious.

"Because, we're headed straight into the next town to get this tire fixed, and you'll have to do this all over."

"Oh…right."

Ruth gave a loving duh as she picked up some things to cram in the back seat.

4

"NO GRAVES IN EGYPT"

(EX. 14:11)

The nearest town was, fortunately, only two miles from where the tire blew. Edy noted the blessing, and Ruth used her phone to find a garage not far from the interstate. It was just about lunchtime, and the ladies grabbed some fast food so they could eat while they waited for the repair. Despite her proper bearing, Edy held such fare as a secret guilty pleasure. Ruth, on the other hand, understood its efficiency in circumstances such as those they currently faced, but loathed it overall and always felt sustained without being fulfilled.

Edy was parked in front of the shop, next to a picnic table. For all the bird droppings on the seat planks, the table's surface was surprisingly clean. Ruth made the logical choice to sit up top, showing compassion to the birds by covering some of their shame with her feet. Edy was far too conventional and leaned against the trunk of her car in a standing sit. As they ate, Edy's phone rang. It was an obnoxious meowing ringtone that she had purchased because it was just too cute. Edith Baldy claimed that answering a phone while eating was atrocious manners, but what if it was Geoffrey. Were the plants dead? What if it was Harry? Did he fall? What if it was John? Was he out of cereal? She flipped it open to check the caller ID. Geoffrey had had to set it up to not answer upon opening in case it was a telemarketer or a Jehovah's Witness. It was her brother, Andrew. He had flown directly to their dad's house from London, where he and his wife were visiting some friends. Edy became emotional at the sound of his voice; she hadn't spoken to Andrew since hearing the news. Her younger brother blew it off, saying he was jetlagged, despite having flown west and being an experienced traveler to boot.

"Listen, Edy," he said, in the smug, Jay Gatsby tone he liked to use, "do you have a particular attachment to the clock."

Edy was speechless. Andrew, impatient as usual.

"The grandfather clock in the front room...dad's grandfather clock?"

Edy stammered thirty different words to tell him no.

"MmI was just wondering because the Frendehlsens, my friends in England, were just saying at dinner last night, or this morning, or whatever, that they saw one in Versailles a month ago, and now they simply must have one. I already asked everyone else, and no one wants it. What's your prerogative?"

Edy's mouth was hanging open.

"You're going to catch a fly," Ruth said, chewing.

Edy ignored the joke, and her brother's misuse of the word 'prerogative,' and could only muster, "You want to ship a grandfather clock to England? They couldn't just buy one in Europe somewhere?"

Hostility, envy, and betrayal were all in her throat. Ruth's keen sense picked up on the conversation and she stopped eating.

"Andrew, I have to go. I'm driving."

"I thought you never talked on the phone while—"

Edy flipped the phone shut as tears filled her eyes. Ruth knew without hearing the other half of the call that Edy had just cut him off. *Good for her*, she thought. She stood up to lend her friend an arm.

"No hello, no I'm sorry, just I want the clock.—For someone else."

"Come on, guys," said Ruth, speaking Edy's mind. "What else have they pawned off already?"

Like a bolt of lightning, Edy was jolted out of her thoughts. She hadn't considered it, but what if Ruth was right? They weren't even all together yet, but what if they were already dividing up the estate, scheming together. Oh, she could see it all now. She could see them in their comfy plane seats, first class, no doubt, smugly smirking at the sunlight through their champagne, setting their eyes on all dad's cool stuff. Were any of them actually sad? Did any of them really know why they were coming? Or was it just a 'grab n' go, see ya later' event for them? *Control yourself, Edy. That's exactly the attitude you don't want to greet them with.* Yes, but better to beat them at their own game if that's what they…She stopped herself. She knew they were just getting her worked up, as they had been doing for years. And it wasn't even them getting her worked up, it was her fantasy assumption of them, which could be wrong, she knew. But what if it wasn't?

Just then, the garage man rolled the tire up and announced its repaired state, smiling as though pleased with himself. Edy's face held its stunned visage as he replaced the tire into the trunk. Ruth wrapped up the lunch trash and shot off to the desk to settle up, telling Edy to situate the car because she knew her friend wouldn't trust her with it. Grateful for the distraction, a break from one reality to another, she began delicately reloading her things into the car. Ruth returned promptly to a visibly rattled Edy stressing the pressing essence of time, and they were soon away.

Back on the road, Edy was already quiet. Ruth cleverly engaged her, not wanting her to escape down whatever rabbit hole her worried mind would try to lure her into.

"Where did he get the clock?" was all Ruth had to say.

Edy paused before answering, wise to Ruth's tactic.

"Toledo. We lived there for three years before Caroline was born. Dad found it in an antique shop, while shopping for an anniversary gift."

"Aw, that's sweet."

"Hmm," Edy murmured. "He was supposed to get a tea set."

A quick laugh was shared, and Edy continued.

"Mom always wanted a really nice china tea set. Really, what happened is that Dad waited till the last minute—it wasn't that he forgot, he just procrastinated—and the shop he went to didn't have a tea set, so he bought something that cost waaay more than a tea set, even a nice one, in the hopes that the over expense would show her how sorry he was about it all. I guess it worked because she did really like that clock."

Edy let the story end there as she suddenly saw her

father in the hallway of their house, rubbing wood polish onto the clock's walnut body, humming as he worked. Edy remembered he enjoyed taking care of it, and she suddenly sensed the smell of it in her nostrils. She thought very fondly of her father in that moment and, finding his particular history fascinating, shared it freely with Ruth.

Leonard Fritz Wimmer was born to German immigrants Hans and Ilsa Wimmer. Hans had a knack for street buzz and when political tensions were high in Europe prior to World War I, he was wise enough to flee to America. It was perfect timing, too, since Ilsa was two months pregnant with Leonard's older brother at the time. They gave their children first names that were common in America so as to fit in, but their middle names were purely German so they would always remember their heritage. Arnold Bernd and Sarah Ilsa, along with Leonard "Lenny" Fritz, always struggled for acceptance as well as food since Hans' business ventures were never very prosperous. Known for his stern demeanor and for not having a sense of humor, he spoke often of Germany, missed it terribly, but was resolute in never returning, fearing that war would forever rack his homeland with the shadow of death.

Leonard was drafted into World War II. His older brother was exempt due to a leg injury sustained at school. Leonard enjoyed the military and stayed an extra tour after the war ended. When he returned home, he went to a local florist to buy roses for his sweetheart. Behind the counter was a young Nora Alice, who smiled sweetly at the hero in uniform. Leonard smiled back, and after delivering the bouquet to a woman who's only greeting was that she had recently mailed his Dear John letter, hoping it would reach him before his return, he went back to Finney's Flowers and asked Miss Nora Finney for a date.

After their wedding, Leonard found work where he could. Edy surprised her parents sooner than they had hoped, but they were still joyful. However, because of their financial weakness and traditional views on gender, saving for Edy to go to college never crossed their minds. Yet, as more children came and cultural standards shifted, the Wimmers had a change of heart. Leonard worked hard and got a better job, then an even better job before becoming a car salesman, which is how he made his fortune. He never lavished money on his children, though, giving them instead a modest life. In fact, the younger ones never knew about his wealth until it was time to think about college. With each successive child, they had more money put away. This in particular burned Edy when Caroline was sent to college, busting Lenny's 'girls don't need college' defense. Eventually, he got a job selling foreign sports cars, from which he retired, in a word—rich. This was how he was able to send his last child through the most expensive schooling, and even give him a Porsche when he graduated med school.

All the while, Edith was left out of the family fortune. Deep down, she knew he loved her, but their relationship was different from the others. Perhaps he kept a sort of distance from her because he felt responsible for her hardship. He had failed to provide for her future and maybe some part of him had regretted it, despite Harry having given her a nice life. He had also relied on her as a mother when his wife died, so he bore witness to her strength as she often sacrificed a social life in service to her family. Leonard saw her strength and expected her to always be strong, using her strengths to provide what his money provided her siblings. All in all, Leonard stayed in good contact with Edy and vice versa. She would spend a couple of weeks with him every year, sometimes on a joint visit from one of his other children.

Lenny had been raised Lutheran but said the war had weeded his religion out of him. Still, he had exhibited earmarks of a moral compass. All his children were baptized as infants, and every year he volunteered his whole family to work his church's Christmas tree lot, equating it to church service during the holiest time of the year. He was loose with attendance, though, but a big family Bible was a staple on his coffee table for years.

Edy looked up from the steering wheel and her story and wished the sky weren't so grey; it wasn't helping her mood at all. It had been a terrible first day, between car trouble and sibling trouble, she was ready to relax. Besides, she needed to check in with Geoffrey. She and Ruth had agreed on a driving in shifts approach to the journey, but Edy just needed someone talking to her to keep her mind sharp and alert. Ruth knew that if she didn't sleep while Edy was driving, she would be just as tired as Edy when she decided to tag out. Ruth couldn't sleep in cars anyway, never could, but she was content with long rides. It relaxed her to watch the scenery fly by her window, especially through the light rain that started just then. Despite her idiosyncrasies, she really was the perfect travel companion. For Edy, at least.

Edy had booked their first hotel online back home. Well, sort of. She made the reservation over the phone while looking at the website. It was a fantastic feat for her, amidst all the planning, packing, and fretting, that she had found the time for it. As they exited the highway, Edy began frantically grabbing behind her seat like she was trying to find a snake to throw out the window. She brought up some papers and thrust them at Ruth.

"Here," was all she said.

Ruth made a noticeably miffed look at Edy as she unfolded them. It was directions to the hotel. Three sheets of directions, turn by turn all the way back to Baldy Manor.

"What in the world, Edith?"

Approaching the stop sign, Edith asked Ruth which way to turn. The navigator was still trying to fathom her friend's technological ineptitude, while trying to locate their exact spot in the meticulous itinerary. Edy pressed her when she saw a car coming up behind them. Ruth said left without looking up from her phone.

"What are you doing?" Edy asked.

"Putting the address in my phone. I'm not reading this epic."

"I printed off those directions for a reason, Ruth."

"To make me nuts, no doubt. Relax, Edy, the machines are not out to kill us."

"In half a mile, turn left onto Sikes Boulevard."

"See, Edith. I think it likes you."

Edy did not appreciate Ruth's humor sometimes.

When they pulled into the parking lot the phone led them to, Edy's heart sank. The sign out front said La Pueblita, but Edy specifically remembered on the phone it was called Tres Cabañas. *Sounds like a resort* she recalled thinking. When she voiced this concern to Ruth, the other woman stayed perfectly calm, unlike Edy.

"Well, this is the address on the sheet."

"But it can't be right. The sign is completely different."

"I'm sure there's an explanation, Edy. Can we just go inside and ask if they have your reservation? Hm? Before this rain picks up?"

"But the sign."

"Let's go in."

"But why is the sign…"

Ruth jumped out of the car and headed straight for the lobby.

When she came back a moment later, she ducked down to tersely tell Edy this was indeed the right place.

"But…"

"It *was* La Pueblita, until two weeks ago. They just haven't gotten the new sign yet. Let's go."

"Well, close the door so I can park," Edy said as though Ruth had inconvenienced *her* somehow.

"Just unload the luggage here, and I'll wait for you to park."

"Ruth, there's a space right there close to the building. I'll just park, and we can get our things there. A few extra steps won't kill you. Now, close the door."

Ruth's eyebrows were almost on top of her head, but she bit her tongue and closed the door. *She just lost her father, Ruth. Remember that.*

Edy parked the car and stepped out. Downpour.

Squishing their way into the lobby, the two ladies were not speaking to each other. Edy was desperate to call Geoffrey, though, so she hurried to the front desk. The rain should have scared them off to find other accommodations, but the good Lord, in His wisdom, chose to refine them a little. The clerk first assigned them two separate rooms. Edy almost went through the roof, but Ruth stepped in. Then they were given a room that housekeeping had missed...for some time. Next, they entered a room with obnoxiously loud neighbors. Edy was too afraid to complain anymore, so she sent Ruth down to straighten things out. When she came back with a new room key, she was wearing a familiar smile that told Edy the front desk clerk was probably cowering in a corner.

No sooner had they entered their new room than Edy called Geoffrey to check in. Ruth immediately set to giving a military grade inspection. Geoffrey had fed the cat and watered the lilies. Edith's stomach dropped. He was only supposed to feed the cat. The lilies weren't due for water until tomorrow morning.

"Did you even read the list?" she scolded.

"Maybe John could read it," said Ruth from the bathroom, checking the towel set.

Geoffrey told her it got a little warm that afternoon and he thought they could use a top off. She anxiously set him straight as though he had switched his father's medication. Ruth's eyeroll was audible. Telling his mother he had done the same to his plants at home did not make her feel any better. She tactfully said it was not the same league and would he please just stick to the instructions she left for him. Ruth could just sense Geoffrey's hair greying over the phone, and she gave Edy a look complete with hands on her hips.

After she hung up, she realized she hadn't told him about the troubles of the day, and she felt bad for the upbraiding. *I mean, I did leave him extremely specific instructions, though.* Still, she knew she would apologize. At the moment, she just needed to unwind and process everything. She watched television with Ruth and munched on some snacks they had brought. The race of worries running through her head slowed to a jog, and she was finally ready to sleep.

"Tomorrow will be better," said Ruth, in the mindreading way she had with her friend.

"I know," was the preoccupied reply as Edy switched off the light.

The next morning, Edy was a nervous wreck right from the start. The weather report in Mureau was calling for rain, and since Geoffrey just watered the lilies the night before, they could be drowned by the end of the day. It wasn't fair. The competition was two weeks away, and this was supposed to be *her* year. She had done all the work, learned from her mistakes, and been gracious and patient every time her name wasn't called by the panel of judges. Now, her loyalty to her family had dragged her away from home and from her victory, and she couldn't trust anybody to take care of them properly, and no doubt her siblings were all gathered at that very moment making decisions she had every right to be a part of, trading off their father's possessions like lunchtime in a grade school cafeteria.

Edy stopped herself because her hands were hurting. She didn't even know she had been wringing them. *Why do they get to me so?* She was glad she hadn't asked it out loud because she already knew what Ruth would say. Instead, she bowed her head and prayed for strength and love for her siblings. She thought of Joseph from Genesis. *Now* he *had it rough.* Would her siblings have sold her into slavery, she pondered. Maybe they weren't *that* bad, she reasoned, but they did fluster her.

Ruth emerged from the bathroom, dressed and ready

to 'do work on the breakfast buffet.' Edy was hungry, too, so she smiled and slipped into her shoes. Today would be better, she knew. She just had to stay calm and trust in the Lord. They were only people, just like her, and besides, she was the oldest. Shouldn't they hold her in some sort of esteem? As the one who had done it already. Done what, exactly? She knew they had all done more than her, probably before getting married. *It's not a competition, Edith.* She had to remind herself of that from time to time, but not for many years now. Deaths really do bring out strange and forgotten emotions. She followed her friend out of their room, and as she pulled on the door handle to make extra sure it locked, she looked up at the sky. Her lilies weren't the only ones who were going to get rained on.

It was quiet in the car as the ladies began their day's journeying. Ruth wasn't in her usual warm, gentle mood. The free breakfast at the hotel had been a bit of a letdown. It wasn't a buffet, as she had thought. It was Edy who'd misled her, so she didn't make a fuss. Still, she was hungry and hoped to put a dent in the kitchen. Perhaps lunch would be better. As for Edy, she was, for lack of engagement, left to her thoughts. The windshield wipers were on a medium intermittence, and each swish of the blades swept a different worry into focus. Ruth randomly, and abruptly, broke the silence.

"Are your headlights on?"

"Yes," Edy answered without looking at the dash, as was her reflex.

Once Ruth had spoken, it was though returning to silence would be some sort of faux pas, so she quickly started a conversation, asking about funeral arrangements. It wasn't the cheeriest topic, but a necessary one. Edy made a grumpy sound.

"Oh, I'm sure they're discussing that right now. Whatever's cheapest and quickest, no doubt."

Under different circumstances, and certainly if it were anybody else, Ruth would be annoyed at such childish sourpussing. She wanted to speak but paused. She had to be delicate; Edy was mourning, but she also liked to defend people who wronged her. Ruth asked Edy what *her* thoughts were about her father's funeral. Edy softened her neck before answering.

"Mom's buried in Woodbriar Cemetery. Dad has a plot next to hers."

Edy twisted her hands on the wheel before continuing.

"I think cremation is the only biblical way to go, though."

Ruth ignored the irony of Edy advocating cremation after she had just scoffed at the idea of her siblings doing it out of cheapness and balked for a different reason. Edy's tone changed, as it always did when she was defending Scripture.—Or at least when she thought she was.

"For you are dust, and to dust you shall return."

Ruth couldn't resist a chuckle.

"What do you think happens to the bodies in the cemetery? They don't stay flesh forever. Or for very long even. You think you slap together a pine box and call it a coffin, and it will just magically preserve a body till the end of time?"

"Well…no."

"I can't condone cremation anyway. 'You were made in His image and likeness.' And you're going to destroy that? That can't be good in my book."

Edy stiffened her neck again with her nose turned up but didn't say anything. Agree to disagree.

The windshield was getting runnier, and Edy turned up the wipers one click. She said a quick prayer in her heart for protection of her lilies. *Meowmeow meowmeow* came the muffled cry from Edy's purse. It was really only annoying if she didn't answer right away. Unfortunately, she never answered her phone while she was driving. Ruth offered to answer it for her; after all, what if it was Geoffrey, or Harry, or the cat? Edy still said no. Ruth supported her friend's decision to not phone and drive, but when there was someone else in the car, and if it might be important…

"Just let me get it, I'll put it on speaker."

"Oh," Edy groaned, "I can't stand when people leave their phone on speaker."

She looked out the window at a sign for a tourist attraction. There were sights she wanted to see, but she planned to visit them on the return trip when time allowed. *Meowmeow meowmeow.*

Ruth grabbed the phone out of Edy's purse and answered it with speakerphone.

"Edith? Hello? Is that you?"

It was her brother, Stuart, speaking from an anxiety that made Edy look like a picture of serenity at any given time.

"Yes, Stuart, I'm here."

Edy gave Ruth a sour look. Ruth smiled at the rain-battered windshield.

"Edith, where are you? Why aren't you here yet? We need you here."

"Stuart, it's a three-day trip. We should be there late tomorrow."

"You drove? Why'd you do that? Why didn't you fly? Who's we?"

"My friend Ruth came with me, and she doesn't like to fly, Stuart."

"Good Lord, Edith. What a poor baby."

"Sounds like the pot calling the kettle black to me," injected Ruth.

"Edith, am I on speaker?"

"Stuart, I'm driving right now."

"And it's raining," said Ruth.

"Edith, please hurry. There's a lot to do."

Ruth was getting impatient.

"Is that all you called to say?"

"Ruth, please. Stuart, we're on our way. I can only drive so much in a day. We should be there late tomorrow."

"Edith, Tommy set up the funeral for Monday. Will you be here by then?"

"She said we'll be there tomorrow," said Ruth.

"Ruth, if you don't mind," answered Stuart assertively.

Edy was once again kicked in the teeth by one of her siblings.

"What do you mean he set up the funeral? Where? Nobody called me."

"I'm calling you now, deary," he said smugly. "It's at Everspring, Monday at one."

"I can't believe he would do that, I…I…"

Ruth could hear tears coming.

"Okay, Stuart," interrupted Ruth, "we're driving, and it's raining, and we'll get there when we get there."

Sensing the slamming flip of his sister's phone coming, Stuart began to stammer, but Ruth held her ground.

"No, no, Stuart, we'll see you all tomorrow. Bye bye now. Sorry for your loss."

Flip!

It seemed Edy would wring the steering wheel in half.

"Edy, pull over if you need to."

"I just don't understand these people." She began to sob. "I never have."

Ruth comforted her.

"It's okay, sweetie, just forget about them for now."

Ruth couldn't help feeling a little worried about Edy falling to pieces on the highway in a rainstorm—with her in the passenger seat. She'd known her too long to be ignorant.

Edy prayed aloud for strength and pulled herself together with her jaw set.

"What was the name of that funeral home, do you remember?" she asked.

"Everspring, I'm pretty sure."

Edy had questions and she knew she would get further with the funeral home than with her own siblings. She thought she might start crying again, but she was too mad. Ruth put on some music low, knowing that Edy liked the sound of rain beating against a car but didn't want it to be the only sound. The AC was on inside, but outside the temperature wasn't dropping despite the weather. Edy was angry; grieving her dead father, and the people who'd survived him were acting downright shamelessly. Why did it have to be raining? It slowed her down, and if she didn't get there as soon as possible she'd end up just another attendee at the funeral. This was her father. It was their father, too, but it was *her* father. She wanted him to be honored in a way that honored Christ, even if he wasn't the most devout believer. What did they know about choosing a celebrant? She knew they would just pick someone out of the yellow pages. Edy Baldy gripped the steering wheel a little tighter, frustrated and wanting to speed up but respecting the water beneath her tires. Ruth always knew what to do in these moments; she would counter Edy's stress with deliberate relaxation. So, she opened a bag of candy while looking out the window, perfectly content to watch the road keep sweeping by.

5

"THE MORSEL EATEN"
(PROV. 23:8)

The rain had let up, coming down now a trickle compared to earlier. Just a lazy sprinkle that was almost relaxing. The mood inside the Baldymobile had lightened as well. The ladies were talking about salvation, having long forgotten the bumper sticker or billboard or whatever that triggered the topic, and Ruth asked her friend if her father was saved. Edy flexed her grip on the wheel, but her eyes never left the road.

She looked very contemplative, but the truth was that it was difficult for her to talk about her father's salvation. The fact that it was difficult for her to talk about it made it even more difficult. Edy wanted to avoid thinking about it. She wanted to believe he'd been a believer, for obvious reasons, but she knew that didn't make it so. If the answer was yes, shouldn't it have come out of her mouth quickly and confidently? If there was difficulty, there was doubt. But who really knows about anybody besides Jesus? The fact that her father wasn't a street corner evangelist didn't mean he wasn't saved. Also, she hadn't been with him in his final moments; if he wasn't saved prior, he could have become so with his last breath. Still, the uncertainty was bothersome to her. If he wasn't, she had to accept that. God is holy, and holiness cannot water down to fairness. Regardless, there were no words that could make her feel better about it. God knew what it was like to be human. He knew that sometimes there just wasn't anything to say, no words to salve a wounded heart. Perhaps that's why Job's friends said nothing for an entire week. What words exist to replace a loved one lost? How bitterly the Lord must have wept at the tomb of His friend Lazarus. Healing doesn't mean there isn't pain. Healing reminds us of what not hurting feels like. A broken heart can't be mended by words.

"I don't know," she finally answered, "but it doesn't help that I'm the only one in the family who cares about it."

"Well," she corrected herself, "I'm sure Geoffrey does."

Ruth always smiled whenever Geoffrey's name came up. She had watched him grow up and was proud of what he'd become. He was very helpful to his mother, but Ruth always speculated that his wife wished he were less so. She loved Amy as much as she did Geoffrey—as did Edy—and she always let Geoffrey know how blessed he was to have her.

Amy Lynn Baldy was from Colorado, and originally surnamed Hamlin, a family known there for raising horses. Even from an early age, she had no interest in the family business and knew only so much about the beasts as to sound smart at dinner parties. She was not a snob but had a properness about her that was often mistaken as such by less refined individuals. She took being a pastor's wife very seriously, but not to appease the naturally watchful eyes of church folk. She aimed to please her husband in this regard, and that in order to please the Lord. She got along well with Edy, but she was still only human. A mother-in-law is a mother-in-law, and hers was Edy Baldy. God love her, she was a good sport in the last name game. Having been overweight in high school, "Hamlin" had bred a resentment within her after some obvious yet brutal teasing at the hands of her crueler classmates. How fitting that she would marry a man who knew the pain intimately. Unfortunate, though, since she had to share that pain till death did them part. She never voiced it aloud, but she did, in fact, wish Edy would call on her husband less frequently.

Edy defended herself to Ruth.

"I don't *make* Geoffrey do anything."

"Well, you ought to *make* John do more."

"How? He's a grown man."

"Who's living in *your* house," said Ruth, with a shocking disbelief that she was the only one who understood the disfunction.

"John does everything I ask of him," Edy rebutted with absolute conviction.

"Why don't you ask him to do more?"

"Geoffrey's just more intuitive about certain things."

"How hard is it to water plants and feed a cat?!"

Edy didn't answer, and Ruth knew she didn't like this topic. She couldn't budge on her opinion, but she softened her tone.

"I just don't understand it, Edith. Geoffrey's married and has his own life. John's single and still living at home."

Edy was still silent, and Ruth sighed her frustration away.

"Is it lunch time yet?" she asked.

Edy was happy for the diversion and shifted in her seat, leaning forward with renewed focus so she would see the restaurant that was getting ready to jump out onto the interstate in front of them. Her senses tagged in, and she was ready to eat. Ruth was on her phone searching for the upcoming drive-thrus, but Edy poo-pooed the idea. She needed a break from family strife and the mundanity of fast food. It was at that moment she noticed a road sign advertising The Farmer's Wife, a local restaurant proudly serving home fare. Edy felt a nice big meal would take her mind off everything and reset her mentality to continue ahead. Normally, Ruth wouldn't turn it down, but she was obligated to voice her objection. Edy also liked the idea of a unique eatery she couldn't find in Mureau Heights.

"But it takes longer," Ruth said.

"Yeah, but we can eat at a chain anytime, any*where*."

"I thought getting there was priority, and on the way *back* we'd take our time."

Ruth didn't want to get Edy riled up again, so she agreed.

The restaurant was less than a mile from the highway. As they pulled into the parking lot, both ladies felt the hair on the back of their necks stand up. The outer aesthetic of the building was clever enough, resembling a classic red barn with white trim. This façade was juxtaposed by the glass, double front doors, but their attention was caught by the liquor store right next door. It sat awkwardly close, like meeting someone new at a party who forgoes the middle sofa cushion. Ruth looked around to count the cars. She couldn't see the back of the building, but she hoped the staff was parked there. Ruth gave her friend a stern, *are you sure?* look, and Edy forced a smile.

"Shall we?"

Ruth wanted to answer *Must we?* but held her tongue. Just as they approached the door, a police car—siren screaming—went flying down the street behind them. Another look from Ruth, and they crossed the threshold. Edy's feet immediately stuck to the floor of the foyer, and she winced. The decorations were appropriate: lots of wood, checkered tablecloths, and an oversized cast iron skillet above the kitchen entrance, drawing the eye of newcomers. As they waited...and waited to be seated, Ruth grabbed a menu to read, silently kicking herself for not looking up reviews of the place, which was her usual practice for first visits.

Finally, a thin young girl came out from the back, giving no start at seeing customers waiting. She seated the ladies and said she would be right back to take their order. Edy turned away, eyes bulging. Such a break in protocol to be sat by your waitress. She commented to Ruth about the girl's brown complexion. Edy Baldy wasn't bothered by skin color, but she was from a different time when a thing different was called out simply for not being the same. She didn't really care, except that she was big on atmosphere, and she had imagined she would walk in and see a team of servers in full colonial dress, all capable of flipping a tractor tire. The farmer's wife must have adopted this tiny thing, God bless her. Ruth looked down at the place setting, irritated that she couldn't have counted the spots on the silverware with just her two hands.—Or Edy's. She looked up to give Edy another winning frown, but her friend was studying the menu. Ruth observed her for a moment, reassessing the situation. Edy *had* just lost her father, whom she had a complicated relationship with. On top of that, her siblings, who had also just lost their father, were acting cold and aloof. Then there was her home life, which Ruth couldn't turn a blind eye to. The crowning cherry on this sloppy life sundae was that she had left her flowers, in capable hands, yes, but at a crucial time, just weeks before they would be judged. Ruth knew how hard Edy had worked on them and could truly appreciate the investment. And they *were* beautiful flowers; Ruth knew she had an incredibly good shot at the victory she had been chasing for years. So what if this wasn't the best meal she ever ate? She'd had other disappointing lunches. Lord willing, it wouldn't be her last.

Just as the greeter-slash-waitress returned, Edy, still deep in thoughts of all sorts, some of which were food, noticed a surge of light in the reflection of the thick and slightly greasy plastic that protected the old, worn menus.

"Have you ladies decided on anything?" asked the young lady.

Edy turned, hoping to catch a peek at the sun that had eluded them for two days now, but just barely made it in time to see the brightness fade quickly back to grey. She concealed her disappointment, locking eyes now with the server, and asked if anything came cooked in the giant skillet on the wall, punctuating her question with abrupt laughter. The woman—Sarana, according to her name tag, which was the only way they knew her name—mustn't have gotten the joke. Edy ordered a dish called The Sunrise Hoedown and set her menu back down on the table. Turning to Ruth, Sarana was met with a look that made no effort to conceal her feelings. Choosing not to point out that they hadn't been given water yet, she ordered a turkey sandwich with fries and handed her menu directly to the clueless waitress.

Not caring if she was out of earshot, Ruth explained her choice. Edy smiled, noting the familiar tactic. Ruth ordered a turkey sandwich whenever she wasn't confident in a restaurant's staff because it could be served hot or cold. That way, if they took their sweet time, she could still enjoy it. She also ordered unsalted fries, guaranteeing they would be fresh and not the ones sitting under a heat lamp. It was a trick she had learned in high school when she worked at such an establishment. Ruth, knowing Edy was most burdened at the moment with family stuff, started talking about the gardening club.

"Any idea who's on the judges panel yet?" she asked.

"No. Janey Jacobson, no doubt. She does it every year."

"Yeah."

"Buckles has been acting strange this year. Well, stranger than usual. I wouldn't put it past him to slither his way up there."

Edy was referring to her obnoxious neighbor, Claude Bucknut. She'd nicknamed him Buckles years ago to take some of his sting out so she could tolerate him. There wasn't anything personally offensive about him, but she wanted to tattoo Leviticus 19:18 across his forehead so she wouldn't just rip his tiny little moustache right off his face.

"Oh, no, I don't think so. Not until he's won one," Ruth brought her back. "He wants it too bad. Judging, for him, would be a way of wagging his tongue at everyone who lost to him, holding it over their heads. It won't mean anything to him until he's got a victory under his belt. He's got something to prove, that's for sure."

In these moments, Edy saw a side of Ruth that most people didn't even know existed. She was a chess player that didn't play chess because it would lower her to her opponent's level. She was shrewd and had the ability to be calculating, but she didn't feel it was useful to the Lord, so she kept it in check. Edy admired that about her friend, that she could see people that way, almost see inside their minds. She knew she couldn't, of course; she just understood people in a unique way. Edy sometimes wished she could do it, but she thought she might use it manipulatively and understood that for that very reason God had seen fit not to give her that ability. It humbled her to see God's perfect design in action. It always reminded her of Paul's first letter to the Corinthians. It took many parts to make up a body, and a foot was just as important as an eye.

When Edy saw Sarana coming with their food, she looked to Ruth, expecting her to be steeling herself for what was about to be laid in front of her. She didn't need Ruth to tell her that she didn't want to eat here. The plates were distributed, and both women were pleasantly surprised by what they saw. Edy's big breakfast for lunch looked very hardy, and Ruth's sandwich appeared full of fresh ingredients. Edy prayed for the meal, thanking God again for Ruth's companionship on the journey. As they ate, neither of them was blown away by their meals, but neither felt disappointed. It was good enough to ignore the nearly empty dining room and the loose professionalism of the employees but not the hodgepodge of concerns on

Edy's mind. What it lacked in therapeutic umph, she simply substituted with the joy of a meal she didn't have to cook.

After she paid the check, leaving a tip she felt reflected the service, but still a tip no less, they hurried out the door. It had cost them an hour, but overall, it was a pleasant pause in the Wimmer affair. Ruth sighed as she opened the passenger door.

"Well, if I'm ever in…wherever we are…again, and needing a turkey sandwich, I wouldn't rule it out."

No sooner had she touched down in the seat than a raccoon appeared from around the liquor store side of the building.

"Thank you for lunch," she added flatly, staring at the furry vagrant.

Edy trapped a giggle in her throat as they drove away, back toward the interstate.

With The Farmer's Wife a few hours behind them, the road was a bit lonely. The rain had taken its lunch break the same time as Edy and Ruth and was sluggish in getting back to work. This was to Edy's favor, though, as a light rain usually proved relaxing for her. The sky was a whitish grey, with no cracks in it for blue to show through. Ruth was in what she called a waking doze, what the preceding generation called 'resting my eyes.' Edy was enjoying the music playing, but it felt a little stuffy inside the car. She fingered the knob just to make sure the air was on. Rain and humidity could sometimes throw off the cooling system, she knew. The taste of bacon lingered in the back of her throat, and she was keen to savor it. She was physically sated and should have felt at ease. Yet, she didn't.

Thomas had a lot of nerve planning—no, scheduling—a

funeral without her. She knew there was no thought, no care, no effort to properly honor their father. He probably had looked at a brochure for a few minutes and then simply picked a cookie cutter package as mechanically as picking a value meal off the menu of a drive thru burger joint. What kind of flowers came with the number two with cheese, she wondered. What about music? What about a photo collage? She was getting ahead of herself, she knew, but she was so upset. Oddly, Thomas, though her closest sibling in age, was probably the furthest from her emotionally. He was the oldest *boy*. It wasn't the first time he had stepped in and acted as the firstborn. It always infuriated her. She was the oldest; it should've been her making the arrangements, planning the service where she would say goodbye to her father forever. So, why hadn't she? Because they weren't all together. She felt it was something they should all do together—with her at the helm. She *was* the oldest. That's all she ever wanted with her siblings, to feel like part of the family, like a member. Like she belonged. She began to weep but didn't want to disturb Ruth. Maybe it was the substitute mother in her, but she always viewed them as a group, and they were collectively separate from her. They all did their own thing, acted on their own, and she often felt like all they had in common was their last name.

Edy looked down at the knobs again. Was the air working right? She felt warm and put a hand up to her forehead, which came back damp. She was almost tempted to switch seats with Ruth. She wiped the hand on her pants and held it up to the vents. The air was comfortably cool, but she still felt uncomfortable. She looked over at Ruth, who was motionless, and cracked her window. The burst of highway noise shooting into the car jolted the passenger, and she feigned alertness.

"What happened?" she asked.

"It feels stuffy. I need some air flow."

"Is the air still on?"

"Yes, but it doesn't seem to be helping."

"Well, turn it up maybe."

"Then it'll get too cold."

"Would you rather be soaking wet?"

Edy rolled her eyes. Even when only half in the conversation, Ruth's wit could be overdramatic.

"How far is it to our hotel?" Edy inquired.

Ruth made an annoyed sound but sprang to action. Shifting in her seat, she pulled out her phone and searched navigation. Ruth had been very insistent on booking their next hotel. She would not be a freeloader, she told Edy, but actually she refused to have a repeat of the fiasco at La Pueblita.

"It's still about two hours away."

Edy groaned.

"I told you we shouldn't have stopped for a long lunch."

Suddenly the lingering taste of food wasn't so savory. And why *was* it so hot in the car? Edy broke down and kicked up the fan a notch. How perfect that the rain started picking up again. Ruth left the navigation screen lit on her phone and placed it in a cupholder in the center console so Edy could follow the directions, and then shifted back into a resting position in her seat. Edy's brow began to tighten, as it always did when she started to search for things to worry about. She started thinking about her flowers. She hoped it wasn't raining this much back home, and that Geoffrey was sticking to her instructions. She had asked Ruth earlier to check the Mureau Heights weather forecast while they were waiting for their food to arrive at the restaurant, but she wouldn't do it. She told Edy she needed to relax and take a break from her troubles for five minutes. When Edy asked her again after five minutes, Ruth had just scowled across the table without moving. Edy wondered if she should get a smartphone so that she wouldn't have to live under technological oppression.

The rain continued to get heavier and heavier, and the windshield was harder to keep clear. Edy was straining to see the road, only...she wasn't sure if it was the rain or her eyes, but things seemed...blurry. She looked down at the speedometer. She stared for a moment. She could see the needle hovering around 45 mph, but her understanding of it was sluggish. Was it good or bad to be driving that speed? She didn't notice anyone passing her, and she looked in her rearview mirror. There was only one car behind her, but back a ways at a safe distance, so perhaps it was an appropriate speed. She looked over at Ruth, who was looking very unsettled and had sweat on her forehead but remained quiet with her eyes shut. She brought the back of her hand to her forehead. Sweat met her touch yet again. Again, she held it up to the vents; they were blowing ice cold. She looked at Ruth's phone. The exit for their hotel was coming up. She felt relieved—and nauseous. So nauseous. What was going on? *Edith Wilhelmina Baldy, pull yourself together!* She shifted jerkily in her seat to rock renewed vigor into herself. She felt miserable, there was no other word for it. It was raining cats and dogs, her siblings were terrible, and her lilies were probably floating in her garden right now, but she knew she shouldn't grumble. Jesus didn't like grumbling. She was getting a free car wash, her best friend was keeping her company, and even if their lunch venue wasn't in the spruciest part of town, she had still enjoyed a nice, big...

Oh, no! Her eyes opened wide. Could this trip get any worse? After everything they had already endured, now they were going to suffer the torment of—

"FOOD POISONING!!!" Ruth sprang to life and dropped her window like she was blowing the hatch on a submarine. The roar of the road sounded like opening an airplane door at 30,000 feet. Her hair was graciously tossed out of the way by the wind as she left her so-so turkey sandwich out on the interstate for the rain to wash away. Edy signaled her exit as the now unwelcome taste of bacon returned in her throat.

6

"STRENGTH OF THE POTSHERD"

(PS. 22:15)

The storm was over. The rain had stopped. The earth was wet, and the air was refreshingly cool but muggy. The sky was white, like parchment paper, appearing even brighter when contrasted against the southern sky. The darkness had only been gone about an hour, but the world in its wake was glad to be rid of it. The plants outside the Valley Inn & Suites were dripping lazily as the gutters poured the excess water down the spouts. It was a typical, uninspired hotel landscape, but the greenery was more vibrant in the way the after-rain calm always makes plants look.

In the lobby of the hotel, the elevator dinged, the door opened, and a very disheveled Edy Baldy came out and headed toward the sundry shop. Her purse hung low, almost to the floor, as she barely possessed the strength to carry it at all. She trudged across the lobby, the picture of misery.

It was the height of embarrassment for her to be seen this way in front of people, and she felt every eye upon her as she crossed the floor. There were, in fact, only two people present besides herself, and neither one was looking at her. It didn't matter, though. In her disoriented state, she perceived them gawking, and what was worse she felt they all knew of the horrors that had transpired in her room. Randomly, she remembered something in the car that she wanted and changed her direction.

The automatic doors belligerently gave a split-second delay before opening, much to Edy's resentment. The outside air hit her, and she wanted to move quickly to get back inside. She was distantly impressed that she even knew where she had parked, but she couldn't imagine what a sight it must have been to see them arrive. It had been pouring at the time, and Edy screeched to a halting stop in front of the building, rushing to check in as quickly as possible so she and Ruth could get to their room and begin to get it over with. After parking and grabbing the lightest piece of luggage they could each carry, they took a side entrance in case the ailment got angry.

As she opened the trunk of her car, she paused intensely. Ruth had left her window down. Edy stared at it a moment, expressionless. There was nothing she could do about it now, and it didn't look like it was going to rain again soon. Maybe it would dry on its own. Maybe the sun would finally make an appearance. Or maybe the car would suddenly burst into flames; that would take care of it. *No need for pessimism.* She grabbed what she came for and went back inside. Walking through the jerky doors, she suddenly didn't know why she had brought her purse anyway. It served no purpose other than to punctuate the pitiful shred of composure she was mustering at the moment. She picked up a few personal items intended to bring her and her friend back to life. Poor Ruth was sleeping the half sleep of food poisoning when Edy left the room. As she approached the front desk to charge the items to the room, the clerk was very friendly.

"Wasn't it glorious to get a few hours of sunshine this morning before that second wave hit?"

Edy stared a dagger through the woman before lifting the corners of her mouth begrudgingly.

Back in the elevator, she shook her head, thinking about the clerk's comment. *Of course it did.* Surprisingly, it was the relaxing elevator music that made her stop and reflect. God really had blessed them in all this. He gave Ruth the prudence to book the hotel when she did, and the pluck to choose a nice one. He had carried them to their destination before they became incapacitated, and safely, considering the weather conditions were less than ideal. It was the unsavory side of life, the one that always made Edy quick to point people to the effects of sin on the world—when it affected someone else, of course. Still, she knew they had never been left nor forsaken.

Just as she entered the room, Edy became aware of how disconnected she was from everything, the way a bewildering illness does. She almost forgot why she had left the room to begin with. Edith Wilhelmina Baldy felt far away. Their departure from Mureau Heights seemed so long ago, and even The Farmer's Wife had already become a memory instead of just yesterday. A breath of home hit her, which she ignored as anyone would feeling the way she felt and taking home for granted as people often do. The place was a shambles, not as it really was, but what they had made of it. Suitcases were open and strewn, shoes were scattered, pillows were on the floor. Fortunately, nothing...off-putting was anywhere other than where it should be. A renewed, albeit sympathetic, compassion came over Edy as she saw Ruth asleep. It was ironic that they were sick in a nice hotel they couldn't enjoy, but in the midst of that irony there was Providence. Surely the experience would have been worse in a crummy hotel. She imagined neighbors banging on the walls demanding they keep the noise down, or breaking the crust on one eye just in time to see a cockroach racing across the pillow, or a window unit stuck on extreme heat, and she was—somewhere in her lagging mind—thankful that these fanciful scenarios were only the conjurings of a frazzled brain. And thankful again for Ruth, the kind of friend who would never pick a place like that.

Edy sat on her bed with her back to Ruth and suddenly felt rejuvenated. The fresh air, however humid, must have done her good. She thought she could pass for a living, breathing, human being, instead of a zombie film antagonist. Though she had been very quiet, Ruth stirred and rose from her rest. She stretched long and hard, as unflattering as a bear after sleeping for three months in a cave.

"Is it over?" she asked in a very bedraggled voice.

"I think so."

"The Lord is good."

"The Lord is good."

Ruth noticed Edy's purchases.

"What did you get?"

"You left your window down."

"What window?"

"In my car."

"Did it rain?"

"It poured."

"Great. Well, the sun should dry it...some."

"We already missed the sun for today."

"Well, Edith, I'm sorry, I wasn't quite myself, I barely remember getting here. At least I shut the door. I did shut the door, right?"

"I got us some electrolyte drinks and granola bars. I also grabbed a clear soda and some travel tissues."

"Electrolyte drinks?"

"Yeah, do you want blue or purple?"

"Such a choice."

Edy tossed the blue one onto Ruth's bed and felt all the strength she had regained leave her in one quick motion, like trying to quick charge a dead cell phone that wasn't turned off. It doesn't get any stronger, it just keeps it from dying, something Edy wasn't opposed to doing at the moment.

Picking up her phone, Edy saw a few missed calls. One was from Thomas, the brother who had usurped her authority; she was not talking to him right now. One was from Geoffrey; if it were anything disastrous, he would have left a message. The last was from Katrina Alberwitz, a fellow gardener she occasionally shared botanical insights with. No doubt that was the purpose of her call. Edy knew she was in no shape to speak with her today. Setting the phone back on the bedside table, she looked at her purple bottle of sugar and then opened the soda. She raised the can halfway to her face but quickly remembered she had only bought one for the purpose of sharing it with Ruth. Slowly, she dragged herself off the bed to get one of the styrofoam cups the hotel had provided for the in-room coffee maker; hopefully, they had not all been destroyed in the frenzy.

Ruth took a slug from her sports drink and exhaled a burst of grief, as though the elixir were a shot of adrenaline. She sat a little straighter, and even Edy could see a little more color suddenly in her cheeks.

"You know, I think we should do something about this."

"What do you mean?" asked Edy, swirling her cup in small circles, as though judging viscosity in a competition for world's greatest clear soda.

"I think we should call somebody. The news, maybe…a lawyer, or even…the police!"

It was an odd role reversal, the kind of thing Edy would be expected to say, but this time she was the voice of reason.

"Well, those complaints never go anywhere, unless every person who ate there yesterday reported the same fiasco. You can't really *prove* food poisoning."

Ruth didn't like being on the receiving end of anyone's negligence; she didn't take it well.

"Well, they should be exposed."

"Ruth."

"I mean it. I could write a letter. Somebody needs to know."

"Somebody?"

"Everybody!"

Edy opened a granola bar slowly, almost reluctantly.

"I think we should get a little food in our stomachs, make sure we can keep it down, and continue resting. Leave out in the morning."

Ruth harrumphed as Edy tossed her a granola bar. She thought she could hear her friend continue her imputation, but she wasn't paying attention. Tomorrow, she would face them. How long had it been? So much to say, so many thoughts racing through her mind, she felt scared again. They would all gang up on her, she just knew it. They always did. At the moment, though, she didn't care.

"Into the lion's den."

"What?"

"Nothing. I'm just thinking out loud."

Ruth stopped talking. She knew when Edy Baldy thought out loud it was because what she was thinking was too heavy to keep inside. She was still mad at The Farmer's Wife, but she would say no more about it. At least for today, but she was going to look it up on her phone. She would leave a scathing review—somewhere—and she would tell everyone she encountered to steer clear. Edy found the tv remote and turned the set on. Sitting on the edge of her bed, chewing her granola bar, her eyes quickly darted to the window and back to the screen. She found a sitcom she liked and relaxed her shoulders a bit as she turned up the volume a couple of clicks.

The next morning, the ladies were in the elevator. Ruth was in high spirits. A good night's sleep had revived her, and she was ready to put a dent in the (confirmed) breakfast buffet. Their luggage was already in the car. They would replenish their bodies and hit the road. A generous tip awaited the housekeeping staff, despite the fact that Ruth had done much of their job for them. She teased Edy for being overdramatic when she suggested they make a pact, swearing never to mention the sounds that took place under duress of their affliction. As the elevator was approaching the ground floor, Ruth could suddenly smell the food that was in wait for her. The ding may as well have been a pistol shot at Churchill Downs. She gave a giddy look to Edy and left her friend in the dust.

Food poisoning is a special class of illness. Due to its mysterious yet violent nature, it stands alone among the many well-known pathologies in the world. It would be an exaggeration to call it a trauma, but whatever the closest thing to a trauma it can be called, it is most definitely that. And like any normal…whatever it is—large bit of unpleasantness… it is just absolutely awful to have to face it alone. However, if in fact you are blessed to share it with someone, and in such close quarters as Edy and Ruth did, you indeed have a friend for life. And if the sufferers are already friends—great friends, even—well, a burst of, say, jubilation after it's over is hardly avoidable. Edy and Ruth were dancing recklessly on the verge of being asked to keep the noise down. The staff—might—occasionally see such behavior—on a Saturday or Sunday morning—from twentysomethings. This, though, this was Monday, and these two ladies were not twentysomethings. Oh really, they weren't being vulgar or offensive, just loud and giggly. The Lord was indeed good, and He blessed their meal and company. Though their bellies were empty, neither of them descended onto their plates. There was some timidity, like an untrusting animal being lured out of safety. Should they taste these rich foods? Would their bodies reject them? The storm was indeed over, and the sun was shining again.—Inside. Outside, the sky was grey and gloomy, the clouds heavy with rain, and the roads ready for another washing. But Edy Baldy and Ruth Krein were having a ball for just a little while.

Once more in the car, the ladies closed their doors almost simultaneously, and the car shook lumberingly one way then the other. It gave them both a quick dose of déjà vu before they settled and clicked their seatbelts. The car was becoming annoyingly familiar to them both. Cabin fever, despite the fact that Edy and Ruth weren't in it *all* the time, was nearing. Such a shame since they just recovered from one illness, would they now fall prey to another? At any rate, Edy grabbed Ruth's hand and started to pray. She thanked God for His hand over their trip, His wisdom, His love, and His perfect will. She asked for His guidance and protection for the final leg of their sending journey. She squeezed her friend's hand on the amen and started the engine. Silver lining, their sinuses and throats were all clear; the air filled their nostrils, and their tongues tasted its bouquet. Bland and moist as it was, they were glad to know it, instead of just knowing it was there.

Meowmeow meowmeow. Not long on the road, and Edy's purse was meowing. The rain had started slow, but the sky said that it was only going to get worse. Edy thought it really would be nice to see the sun. It had been such a dreary trip thus far. As a gardener, she had a healthy and practical appreciation for rain, but for long car rides it took away from her enjoyment of the scenery when there were no breaks in its gloom. After Ruth's last handling of Edy's family, she had elected herself official mediator between her friend and the Wimmer children. She pulled the flip phone from its cave—*When's this thing due back at the museum?*—and looked at the caller ID.

"It's Thomas," she announced.

"Ohhh, I wonder what he wants."

Edy had no sooner spilled the words from her mouth when she jerked forward and grabbed the wheel tightly with both hands. It was only the petitioned protection that kept them on the road and in their lane at that moment, though it did scare Ruth.

"What is it, Edy?"

"We were supposed to be there yesterday."

Her eyes were wide, her face was panicked. Her neck and shoulders tightened. She suddenly remembered the missed call. He was wondering where she was. In the chaos of everything that had happened, it had completely slipped her mind that they had burned an entire day. It had been shuffled into the back of her subconscious, so that she was aware they had a goal, but she didn't know what it was.

"The funeral!"

The realities of their lost time began hitting her in waves.

"Oh, Ruth, do you think they did it without me?"

She began tearing up, and—Ruth to the rescue. Superfriend began shushing Edy and assuring her that of course they wouldn't bury their father without her present, though she only half believed it herself. All the while, the poor cat kept on meowing as Edy processed things.

"Should I answer it?" Ruth asked, her eyes on the road ahead.

Before Edy could respond, the ringing stopped. She sat frozen. Maybe he was worried. Maybe he was calling to make sure everything was alright. They *were* a whole day late. With all the rain, they could have been in an accident. *Edy, don't think like that.* Even in the hypothetical, she scolded herself. Once she explained everything, he would surely be sympathetic. The fact remained, though, he did need to know. They all did. The funeral was in a couple of hours and needed to be called off.

7

"THE OPEN SQUARE"

(JUDG. 19:15)

"Edy?"
"Edy?"
"EDY?"

It was only Ruth's hand gripping Edy's arm that pulled her out of her head.

"I'm fine," she answered finally.

She was far from fine. She was terrified. She felt a film of sweat on her forehead. Was she going to be sick again? No, just nerves. Why was she so scared? It was a pretty big ball that she had dropped—but that wasn't fair. She had been ill—violently ill. She couldn't be expected to be a pillar of leadership and responsibility under those circumstances. Could she? They would say yes, even though if the situation were reversed, it would be a different answer. Plus, they would only consider her their leader when she failed to lead. Any other time, they pushed her aside and took her for granted. Ah, but she was the oldest. That's what they would throw in her face. They would use her own motto against her, just like the serpent used God's command against Adam and Eve. *Stop comparing them to Satan.*

"Edy!"

"WHAT, RUTH!?"

She immediately took a pause and gripped her friend's hand.

"I'm so sorry, Ruth. Please, I…I didn't mean to snap at you."

Ruth was too shocked to be offended. This wasn't like Edy at all. She knew she was under serious strain, and it pained her to watch it, but she would keep doing so because that's what friends do.

"I said, do you want me to drive for a while?"

"No. Call Thomas back.—Please."

Ruth steeled herself. It was a lot for her, too. Carrying half of a heavy load was still demanding work. She handled Edy's phone like she was turning the key on a nuclear launch, solemn yet determined.

"Everything will be fine, Edith Baldy," she assured. "You haven't done anything wrong."

"I know."

As the call connected, Ruth put it on speaker and laid the phone on the center console.

Thomas' 'hello' was noticeably annoyed. Edy jumped into her explanation of what had happened and was met with the callousness she expected. Ruth sat silently, her jaw tightening. If this were *her* brother talking to her like this, he would rue it for sure.

"Did your friend pick the restaurant?" he asked with a tone.

"I don't see how that's important, Thomas, but no, I did."

"Tsk! Figures."

Both ladies rolled their eyes, knowing it would have 'figured' no matter who had chosen the restaurant. He was being combative just for the sake of it.

"Couldn't you just keep a window rolled down in case you got sick again?"

It was a pitiful attempt at a joke.

"No, actually, it's raining. Pretty heavy."

Edy's eyes turned skyward. Despite the downpour, the heavens were quite bright to the north. She knew the sun was there—oh, would she ever see it again? She barely held back the tears in her eyes. This weather was pushing hard against her, she knew she would sound crackers if she started inferring a spiritual battle in the expanse.

"Well, at least you wouldn't have to worry about your car getting dirty."

His frail chuckle was telling of the fact he knew he was in the wrong and being tacky about it to boot. It was at this crack that Ruth hit her limit.

"I think that's quite enough, Thomas."

"Ah, yes. Stuart told me…I assumed I was on speaker." His voice became extravagantly sarcastic. "Hello, Ruth."

Ignoring the intended insult, Ruth commandeered the conversation.

"We hit a snag, but we're en route, arriving this evening, Lord willing. But, of course, today's proceedings will need to be rescheduled. Sorry for the inconvenience, but you sound like you can handle the arrangements, so we'll see you tonight, okay? Okay, then, see you soon. Sorry for your loss."

The phone hit like a thunderclap as Ruth closed it. There was a brief silence, then Ruth took Edy's hand again and gave it a squeeze.

"I don't know how you put up with them, deary."

Edy was still trying to keep the rain in her eyes from flooding the car. Thomas had tried cutting Ruth off multiple times, but she kept talking, pushed on through, held her ground, and then got off the phone. She knew how to handle his type.—Their type. She didn't understand how Edy could have come from the same household as them. Maybe she was adopted. Well, in a way she was, as one of the elect of God. Perhaps that was it. Cut from the same cloth, but she had been dyed red with the blood of Jesus and was therefore of a richer Spirit. They drove on through the rain. Ruth put on some music so they wouldn't have to speak. There was an unspoken mutual desire to be alone with their thoughts. Ruth contemplated the twisted thicket of family, while Edy just prayed in her heart.

When they finally pulled onto Meadow Thrush Trace, where her father had lived for many years, Edy shifted in the driver seat, her shoulders tightened, and she drew a deep breath. Ruth locked eyes on her and shifted as well. Looking down the street, Edy recognized Thomas' car. He defensively called it a truck, but really it was an SUV. 'An *off-road* SUV,' he would always add, demanding you acknowledge the distinction. Either way, Edy thought it was foolish of him to bring the gas-guzzler on the three-hour drive from his place to Dad's, when he had a sedan at home. Wesley's car was blocking the driveway, as was his peculiar custom whenever it was already full. The rest of the vehicles present were all rentals. The street was otherwise busy enough. Edy had to park two houses down. *Typical* she thought. *Why?* she immediately answered herself, trying not to be snarky. Oh, but they could get at her so easily.

She put the car in park. This was it. Time to face her family. It was just her little brothers and sister. So, why did Edy feel as though she were approaching a tribunal? She was so outnumbered; she always had been, and they got all the support, the encouragement, the success…Her thoughts had been so frantic lately. The closer they got to this moment, the more random, the more chaotic, the quicker she arrived at knives drawn any time they entered her mind. This was not going to be easy. It would hurt, Edy knew. The weight of years—some of it fifty years old—was heavy on her, heavier still because she seemed to be the only one who felt it, the only one who cared. Still, they had come a long way…and had been through a lot in four days…

"And it wasn't to put up with their nonsense," Ruth reminded her.

"I know. It was to bury my father."

Ruth smiled.

"While wading the mucky waters of their nonsense," Edy added with a giggle.

"Alright, Edith, settle down," said Ruth lovingly.

Edy shut off the engine and pushed her door open, and Ruth quickly grabbed her hand. Edy looked back to see Ruth's face suddenly very serious. She shifted back towards her friend, who bowed her head. Ruth prayed with gentleness, but with determined words. She always had. It was one of the things Edy admired most about her. She prayed for Edy's strength for the challenge awaiting them inside, she prayed for a spirit of love and understanding for her siblings who she always felt lacked both, and—she reached over and pulled the key from the ignition so the door open dinger would stop dinging—she prayed that He would bring the Wimmer children closer together while blessing the business at hand. After the amen, Edy gave Ruth another thank you look, and the ladies got out of the car. They didn't want to have to walk the two-house distance back to the car to get their things, but they also didn't want to try dragging it all along the sidewalk in a lazy man's load. Besides, there were plenty of people in the house that could help after pleasantries were exchanged. Edy sniffed with a smirk, knowing that 'pleasantries' was the best she could hope for from this lot.

As Edy pushed open the front door, it creaked loudly, as in a horror movie when the killer enters a house. Only in her case, instead of the teenagers being terrified of him, they're just very annoyed at his presence. Not quite the fanfare she had envisioned, but it did turn every head in the house her direction. Yet so many heads seemed to be missing.

"Well, look who decided to show up."

There was what passed for warmth in Thomas' greeting, so Edy ignored it.

"Hello, everybody," she said meekly, hoping for what passed for warmth from the rest of them.

Silence was her answer in the room so dry and static.

"Where's Henry?" she shifted.

More silence.

"Probably wrist deep in somebody's chest," said Thomas.

"I doubt he's coming," said Caroline, completely indifferent, both to her sister and her oldest brother's attempt to gross everyone out.

It was surreal to see them all together, yet it was the silent, lonely presence of Dad's empty chair that captured her attention, with the orange Afghan draped over the back that might as well have been sewn into the upholstery for as much as it ever left that spot. Staring straight at her, it stabbed her heart with a fresh pang of loss. Her eyes quickly looked away to the worthy distraction of the long-disbanded Wimmer gang. Thomas sat on the sofa facing the door. Edy's father had always said it was there for readiness. Ready for what, no one knew. Stuart—who was the only one accompanied by a spouse—and his wife, Claudia, were over by the record table, both with a wine glass in their hand. Caroline was in the kitchen, opposite Wesley, who usually bored her with architecture stories. Andrew was standing in front of the window. He had, no doubt, watched Edy and Ruth walk all the way from the car to the front door, and probably didn't even mention it to anyone. And then, Edy spied the one face in the room that technically didn't belong but was always welcome, and always able to make her smile and feel happy to be seen. Tucked into a corner, with a magazine in her lap, Nancy Sprigger gave Edy the warmest welcome with just a smile.

"Hello, Edith. How're the flowers?"

"Beautiful when I left. I just hope they're still there when we get back."

As Edy answered, Nancy was already walking over to offer condolences and a hug. Tears ran from the eldest Wimmer's eyes.

"And you must be Ruth. It is so nice to meet you finally."

She moved to hug Ruth, who gladly met her kindness and wondered why this woman couldn't have been Edy's sister.

Nancy had lived across the street from Leonard for many years. Friendly from the first day she moved into the neighborhood, she was a sweet woman about ten years Edy's junior. Raised in the South, her accent was all but faded, but her compassion and hospitality were purest Dixie. She worked for the Army her whole life but took early retirement when her husband died suddenly of a heart attack at forty-five. She had a daughter who was working on a master's degree in marine science from, of all places, the University of Texas at Austin. Nancy had become a sort of caretaker for Leonard in the years following her husband's death. She would cook for him, clean up a little, and do laundry. Despite Lenny's insistence that he could do it all himself, he never shooed her away. There was a mutual benefit to her being there. Each enjoyed the other's company, finding comfort in the practical dynamic of a relationship. Chiefly, the 'being taken care of-having someone to take care of' principle. Eventually, her weekly visits became daily visits and indeed it was she who discovered Leonard the morning after he died.

Edy had come to know her well over many visits, and since they were both born again, got along perfectly. Edy seemed to be the only one who appreciated or even approved of Nancy's being around. Whereas she was grateful to have someone so close who could look in on their father, and genuinely enjoyed doing so, her siblings took a defensive stance, wherein their unspoken words called her a meddler and an intruder. She wasn't oblivious to it, either. That's why, when she found Leonard, even though she wanted to call Edy, it was Wesley who was notified because he lived only fifteen minutes away. Plus, her Southern upbringing told her it was best the family hear it from its own.

Edy looked back to her family. The few who were huggers gave their best perfunctory support, while the rest mumbled empty remarks about better circumstances and whatnot. Edy apologized for the delay and acknowledged all the work they had to do, but when she mentioned her and Ruth bringing their things in, the room fell quiet once more, eyes shifted, and the awkwardness was palpable. Once again, Thomas spoke up.

"Well, we're kind of full up here already."

It was the 'we're' that turned Edy's stomach, as though it didn't include her, like she was outside the Wimmer *We*. Ruth's blood turned to lava and her face to lead. Thomas had claimed the master bedroom—*Of course he did, usurper!*—and Andrew was in the guest bedroom. Wesley had offered the inseparable real estate players his spare rooms. Edy's jaw was on the floor, but Ruth was ready to box.

"Aren't you at least going to offer us the manger out back?"

"No manger. There's a shed. Probably gets pretty hot this time of year, though."

Thomas' unfeeling way of saying it put Ruth over the edge. She dropped what she had carried in the same way a gunslinger pushed his coat behind his holster to show he was ready to take a life.

"Now that is just downright—"

"You can stay with me," Nancy blurted out.

Thomas' smirk at Ruth did nothing to soothe her temper, but rather than wipe it off for him, she kept her eyes locked on him and said, "Thank you, Nancy. Edy?"

Edy was lost somewhere far away. Was Harry taking his medication? The right ones at the right times? What time was it there? Had Geoffrey arrived yet to feed Duke? Was this a watering day? Hopefully, the lilies weren't getting scorched in the tauntingly abundant sunshine back home.

Ruth brought her back, and Nancy ushered them to her house, even offering a spot in her garage to the Baldymobile. Picking up her things, Ruth announced, "The Lord save these Samaritan innkeepers!"

It didn't matter the inaccuracy of the statement, none of the Wimmers caught it, but the point was loud and clear. Not that they cared. What really had Edy expected? She had hoped for better but knew who they were. Still in a daze, she followed her escort out of her father's house.

Nancy kept a beautiful home, lived in but neat. Though it was very inviting, Nancy confessed to wishing more people came to stay, or even visit. The only weakness in the ambience was the collection of ceramic Victorian lady dolls. They weren't in excess, but they were all positioned perfectly so as to be unavoidable. The proverbial herd of elephants in the room. It was hard to tell if the dolls were too fancy for the furniture or if the furniture was too homely for the dolls. Whichever it was, the earthenware damsels were most definitely out of place.

But Edy didn't even notice them. This was made odder still by the fact it was the first time she had ever seen them. In all the years they had known each other, Edy had never been in Nancy's house, yet somehow she was unaware of the unorthodox collectibles. Proper as she was, Ruth couldn't take her eyes off them, already fearing she would wake in the night to find one standing by her bed, grinning at her. Right now, though, all Edy could think about was what had just happened across the street. The iciness she was met with—Ruth said what Edy felt but couldn't voice—Edy felt like an intruder. She gave a thin chuckle to herself at Ruth's comment. *Manger—good one, Ruthy.* She was *so* thankful for Ruth; she couldn't imagine how she must feel. If Edy was an intruder…what did that make Ruth? She was embarrassed at how her siblings had treated her. *They hated me first.* She chuckled to herself again, the kind of chuckle that contained no mirth whatsoever in it.

The ladies got settled into their rooms. Edy said a prayer of thanks for Nancy; the woman had been a blessing to the Wimmers for a long time. She hoped Nancy hadn't been bullied at all, but then, she had known them for years, and despite her small appearance, Nancy could handle herself. Of course she could; Ruth, too. Edy was the milquetoast in the bunch, but then they hadn't grown up with those people.

Edy decided to go back across the street to ask about dinner plans, thinking it would be nice to celebrate the reunion. Ruth almost cackled.

"You just can't get enough, can you?"

"I know they're difficult, but they're my family and I haven't seen them all in years."

"I know, Edy, but…" Ruth paused, half 'this poor woman'-half 'do I really have to explain this to her?' "It's been a long day."

"Everybody likes to eat, even if it's with someone they don't like."

Ruth almost started crying *for* her.

"You're coming, right?" Edy asked, with childlike vulnerability.

She felt it was something best left to family only, but

after the "welcome" they had received, there was no way she was going to let her friend sup with these people alone.

"Oh, I suppose I'm okay with sucking another free meal out of you."

"Who said *I* was paying?"

Their laughter was full of love, and surely the Lord was pleased by it. Nancy was invited, too, but declined. She did, however, give them a spare key in case they came back when she was asleep.

The air outside was cool but humid. Edy flattened her face at what that probably meant. *More rain, why not.* It randomly occurred to her that for all the rain they had seen thus far, they had heard no thunder. As ominous as the rain was for a competitive gardener two weeks before showtime, what was a storm without thunder? Walking up the drive, she eyed her father's landscape perfunctorily. She was too distracted to notice it when they first arrived, but now she did a sort of status check, having invested some of her own time on it over the years when she would come to visit. Bless her heart, Nancy had helped to keep it up, too, and Edy's father was fairly attentive to the weeding. It was a nice yet uninspired arrangement of perennials, several of which required little watering. Perfect for an older man who never saw the sense in standing in front of a bunch of plants holding a running hose.

When they entered her father's house again, Edy immediately noticed the mood change. It was lighter—literally, there were more lights on—and there was music playing upstairs and a stirring in the basement. Thomas appeared to see who had come in, and his face said a burglar would've been more welcome company. He explained to them that Stuart and Caroline had already gone to dinner, Wesley had gone grocery shopping on his way home, and he was just downstairs looking over things.

"Andy drew the short straw for a dinner run." He hesitated and added, "I can call him to add something if you…"

'Looking over things'? What did that mean? She knew exactly. Just then she noticed an empty space on the mantle that was once occupied by a hideous objet d'art. It was a metalworking of some sort, no one ever knew what it was supposed to be, and where it came from had probably gone with Dad into the great beyond. But one thing Edy knew: it hadn't moved from that spot in decades, and it was there just an hour ago before she left for Nancy's. So, where was it now? She knew it; she was right all along. They were already divvying up the estate, making deals, lunchroom trading. Without her. The irony was, Edy wasn't even after anything. She just wanted everything to be fair, for the sake of propriety. Plus, some part of her thought it would be fun to do that part together. Maybe she wanted to be in on the lunchroom. She looked toward the hallway where the grandfather clock had resided since her father bought the house. Still there. She rolled her eyes at the thought of Andrew driving off with it sticking out of the trunk of his rental car. Maybe they were beyond reconciling—as a family. It had been this way ever since Mom died. She'd been gone so long; it was hard to remember if she was really the glue that had held them all together.

"That won't be necessary," she said, trying to stiffen up.

The two ladies left to go back to Nancy's, where they had an open invitation to the kitchen. As soon as they were outside, Edy's emotions shifted. She felt humiliated, publicly disgraced in front of Ruth and Nancy. Talk about disappointment. Their father was dead, they hadn't all been together for years, Edy had just battled food poisoning (among other troubles), and all she wanted was to know that she still had a family, that she still belonged to them somewhere in their hearts. But no. It was almost as though they had taken a vote to declare her dead to them, as though the passing of their father was the breaking of whatever frail bond still held them together. Now she would have to handle the tedious business of a familial death, partnered with what were basically enemies, all the while carrying an emotional burden by herself that was meant to be shared. Edy scowled absentmindedly all through the sandwich Ruth had made her. She couldn't stop thinking—about her family, about what she had left in Mureau, about the elusive sun, about everything. What *had* happened to them? And why had nobody besides Stuart brought their spouse? She felt like they were a fleet of ships who had long ago set sail, drifting in different directions. And never returned to port. It was all so rotten she could just spit, but not in Nancy's house. That would be rude.

8

"INTO THE CISTERN"

(GEN. 37:24)

The next morning, Edy awoke…not refreshed but focused. The previous night had given her a heightened awareness that she was going to have to lean heavily on God to get through this ordeal. She was determined to come through it with her Christianity intact. This would be difficult, she knew, because to her siblings, just mentioning her faith made her a fanatic. She realized she might be a little battered and bruised on the other side, but what mattered was that God was glorified by how she handled herself. She was almost grateful for the wakeup call, and she had risen early to read her Bible and pray. She prayed for strength in her role as the eldest, for wisdom to make respectful but practical decisions, patience to remain Christlike when her siblings became difficult, joy to stay aware of God's goodness, and trust to step back and acknowledge the end of her abilities, content that God would take care of *everything* she couldn't. She added a quick prayer for her flowers, and instantly heard a voice inside her ask why the competition was so important to her. She was startled by it. Not because it was the Holy Spirit's, but because it was hers. It wasn't much money at stake, and the glory wasn't lasting, but boy if she didn't want it. Edy looked out the window to see light breaking in the East, and quietly perceived an excitement to think if the sun would come out today.

Before leaving her room, she called Harry to check in. Duke Archibald threw up the day before; it wasn't a lot, looked like hair mostly. In the motherly tone she used with her husband, and pretty much everyone else besides her children, she told him to check the kitty grass. If he was out, plant some new seeds in the sunny window to keep his little tummy settled. Edy then called Geoffrey for a status report on the garden. The flowers were still thriving and radiating beauty. Strangely, she felt no joy—not even relief—at the news. She told him about the cat. Walking past, Ruth heard through the open door.

"Sir Scratch has the hurls, eh? Gross."

Edy scowled as she told Geoffrey the instructions for the lilies that she had written down for him before she left and, presumably, he had been following the whole time.

When she came out of her room, she put Ruth's jaw on the floor by telling her she would go alone. She was going to head straight for her dad's house, thinking that her siblings would have coffee and some kind of breakfast something ready when she got there, but her memory pulled her hair and she decided to at least take a coffee with her. If nothing else, seeing her cross the street with a mug in her hand would be tacky enough to make them all cringe. *Easy, Edith Wilhelmina.* Besides, any other time she would feel the same way. Closing Nancy's front door behind her, she felt the humidity instantly. Another grey day, no doubt. She wanted to look over her shoulder, between the houses, to the East, to see if the light was still there, offering a glimpse of what she hadn't seen for days, but she resolved to keep her eyes forward. If she didn't look, then she wouldn't be disappointed when it wasn't there. If only Lot's wife had been so pessimistic. As she stepped into the road and looked at her father's house, she started thinking about him. She hadn't had a moment since arriving to properly console or be consoled. Fat chance on the latter, she thought, but she couldn't shake the desire to ask them all individually how they were feeling. At least if she asked, she would be able to discern which of them, if any, actually had feelings about their father's death. She wanted to take some time and reflect on him and his impact on each of their lives. She had her Bible with her, too, with some passages earmarked.

When she walked through the front door, the scene was already abuzz with activity. Everyone was busy with something, sorting papers, phone calls, taping boxes. She noticed that none of them were talking to each other or working together on anything. Each person had their task.

"Well, look who decided to show up."

Edy found Thomas' repeat greeting annoying and felt less warmth in it this time. Some of them didn't even look up from what they were doing to acknowledge their sister. She called for their attention, and they didn't hide their irritation very well. She told them what she wanted to do before getting started, which made her squeamish to say since they were clearly already hard at work. The look they gave her made her think she had three eyes.

"That's what the funeral's for," said Caroline, still not looking up.

"Which is now two days away," Thomas made his displeasure known.

"Yeah, but we're not all together," Edy defended.

"Who's not going to be there?" Stuart asked, thinking he was clever.

"I mean we're not *alone* together."

The others sidestepped Edy's idea to talk about the business at hand, selling the house, the holdings, possessions, collections, and so on. They almost seemed to forget she was even there, and that's when Edy did something unexpected.

"I want the car!"

Stunned. Stunned was the only word to describe the faces staring at her at that moment. They acted as though it was crass for her to say so. Perhaps it was, and Edy had no idea why she had blurted out like that. She hadn't been thinking about her father's car, but out it came. If it was a desperate attempt at a power play, she should have just yelled out 'I'm the oldest!' which was the typical defense inside her head. A smirk darted around the room, validating Edy's darker suspicions as she suddenly felt like a wounded animal being surrounded by hungry wolves closing in.

"Well, I've always liked that car," said Stuart coyly.

"Oh, you know how Sheila is about blue cars," said Andrew in his annoyingly giddy way.

"It *is* a fine machine," said Thomas carelessly looking at nothing.

What followed was an utter fiasco, the polar opposite of what Edy had envisioned the day becoming. The anti-Edy band of Wimmers proceeded to pump up the value of the car, which would force their big sister to give a bigger share of her inheritance, but what was odd was how they got caught up in their little charade and began arguing with each other. Thomas already had three cars, Stuart couldn't drive a stick, Wesley always complained about the seat, yada yada yada. Odder still was Edy's resolution to not be left out of it, as though any talking was better than no talking. Sure enough, they ended up yelling at her, too. The hubbub went on for an hour before they all dispersed in separate directions for the day. Edy stormed across the street back to Nancy's, not noticing the darkening sky. She had to stop herself from slamming her host's front door as she pushed back hard against the tears.

Ruth looked up from a cup of tea as Edy stood in the entryway and looked back down again.

"Well, that didn't take long."

"Ruth, pack your stuff. We're out of here."

"No, we're not."

"I've had it with these people."

"Again?"

Edy started choking up, and Ruth finally put down her cup and looked at her friend.

"What happened?"

Ruth's look and tone embodied everything that Edy cherished about their friendship, the way that all the warmth of years was wrapped around the question. How else was it possible for two words to feel like a hug?

Edy began unraveling the events of the morning, and Ruth struggled to listen. She had always been disgusted with all the stories her friend told of the mistreatment from her siblings, but at some point, shouldn't Edy have stood up for herself? It was one thing if they were mean, but if they continued to act that way, shouldn't Edy put a stop to it? She tried to explain this sentiment, but perhaps the timing was wrong.

"Stand up for myself? Really? How?"

"Edy, I didn't mean…"

"Those people are Goliath, but I'm not David."

"Now…"

"You don't know what it was like, Ruth!"

Ruth checked for Nancy, even though she knew she wasn't home yet.

"You don't know what it was like," Edy continued, "growing up feeling unwanted."

Ruth softened.

"They wanted the others, but not me. Gave them everything, even sent them to college. What did I get? A family of educated moneybags that never visit. Oh, they'll visit each other, sure, but they're never knocking on my door. Is that what he taught them? Thanks a lot, Dad!"

"Edy, you shouldn't talk like that."

"Why am I even here? I should've just stayed at home and sent some flowers."

And that just unlocked a whole other door.

"Meanwhile, my own flowers are probably going to be dead by the time I get home, just in time for me to get passed over, a-gain. And is the sun *EVER* going to come out?!"

Edy's whole body was heaving from her excitement. Ruth had never seen such behavior from her friend. She moved in to hug Edy, but the frazzled woman sidestepped her and left the house.

The wind blew at her, and she pressed against it angrily.

Not in the mood, wind. She felt charged like the air before a storm. She wanted to have it out. With God. Edith Wilhelmina Baldy never wavered in her faith, but like any other human being, she had had moments in her life where her finite understanding hit its limit, always to her frustration. Through all the devastation of losing her father and all the anxiety that came from leaving Mureau behind, she had set out on this trip with the anticipation that the situation would bring her closer to the siblings she had always perceived at a distance. Why did she always feel so insecure around them? So embarrassed about every little thing? So inferior? And why had she blurted out that she wanted Dad's car?

She felt a pang of embarrassment at that thought. The sad thing was that they all knew they had no need or want for their father's car. They would sell it lickety-split; they truly were just being slithery. Seeing it manifest hadn't made Edy feel better, though. She didn't need the car either. Still, it was a nice one, and hers wasn't going to last forever; it wasn't as nice as theirs. That's when she felt the Spirit inside, prodding her to say it aloud. She had to push aside her pride because saying it would remind her that she was just as much a sinner as them. She didn't want to be equal to them; she wanted them to be beneath her. After all, she was the oldest. But it shouldn't have mattered to her. She had told each of them before at some point that everyone is equally guilty of sin in God's eyes, but as such, Christ died for all people, offering salvation through forgiveness of sins equally. So, what was the deal? It wasn't greed. She spoke it inside. She knew it wasn't greed. Nice try. They weren't greedy either. She stopped walking and clenched her fists, closing her eyes.

"Envy."

It stabbed her to hear her own voice accusing her. She started crying. Had she ever stopped crying? Between tears and rain, she felt she was drowning. Well, tears, rain, and so much uncertainty. She felt anymore like all she had to do was think about rain and it would happen, and sure enough, looking up, the sky was murky. *Of course it is.* She wished she were at home. She was so worried about her flowers. She trusted Geoffrey to do what she asked, but he didn't have the instincts. She was the only one who could do everything right for them. Why was she thinking about the garden right now? She was furious about everything. The trip was a nightmare, her siblings were awful, and her plants were 2,000 miles away and probably looked like she felt at the moment. She knew she needed to ask God's forgiveness for envying her siblings. As soon as she said amen, it started to rain, and her tears blended with the drops. She felt so alone. She wondered if a random person walking by would stop to notice her, or just fly right past, hurrying to get out of the rain. Even if they did, they'd think she was nuts and hurry by all the faster. Oh well, she couldn't get any wetter, so she headed back for Nancy's.

As she stepped onto the porch, Ruth threw the door open and brought her inside.

"Prodigal fool, are you done slopping around with the pigs?"

Ruth's gruff tone belied her watered eyes, and Edy smiled back but instantly started to sob. Ruth took her friend into her arms and held tightly.

"I know, honey. I know."

While Edy changed into dry clothes, Ruth made tea.

Just as they were sitting down to it, Edy's phone rang. Ruth almost reached for it, knowing a little silence would be golden at that moment. She restrained herself when she saw it was Geoffrey. Edy almost looked relaxed when she answered, but it evaporated quickly. Geoffrey had injured his back and would be bedridden for a few days.

"What about the lilies?!" Edy exclaimed.

No 'how did it happen?' no 'how do you feel?'

"Thanks, Mom," Ruth said behind her teacup.

Edy scowled while Geoffrey made a ludicrous suggestion.

"*Whose* dad?"

"Harry?" Ruth asked with equal incredulity. "Could he even lift the watering can?"

Edy bulged her eyes in irritation, and Ruth coyly went back to her tea.

"John? He doesn't have time for that. Besides, you'd have to teach him how."

Ruth swallowed hard on her *tsk*.

Edy clutched the drapes as she looked out the window at the downpour.

"Is it raining there?"

Geoffrey told her that it was overcast in Mureau, but that there was a solid chance for rain on Friday.

"That's two days from now!" Edy began choking up.

She didn't want her son to hear her cry because it would just upset him, so she put her hand over her mouth while the back of her throat got hot, and her cheeks once again became wet. She told Geoffrey to get better soon. After putting her phone down, Edy prayed for God to heal her boy. But she wasn't sure for whose benefit she was praying.

9

"A GREAT CHASM FIXED"

(LUKE 16:26)

When Edy awoke, she was aware it was morning. Her eyes groggily cracked open to perceive the early light, wandered lazily around the walls and closed again. The room was cold and quiet, but Edy's heart was too heavy to care. She wondered why she was here at all. She should have stayed home, flown out the morning of the funeral, and flown back that evening. She wanted to say that was something her siblings would do, yet here they were, all arrived before her. Well, not *all* of them. *Why didn't Henry come?* she wondered. *What's wrong with that boy?*

Suddenly, a funny thought entered her mind. Nobody had really at any point invited her. She didn't need an invite to her father's funeral, of course, but still. Caroline had called her—*Probably drew the short straw*—but Edy had asked about details and dates and plans and all that. It was clear to her they would have preferred she stay in Mureau Heights, fretting over her flowers and staying out of *their* business. It wasn't just her, though. They had always been a private bunch. None of them had even brought their spouses except Stuart, but only because she was the water to his fishy gills. If he stayed away from her too long, he would dry up and simply expire. At least, that was the way he presented it. Of course, Edy had left Harry at home, but that wasn't the same thing. Fine, if that was what they wanted, she would oblige. She resolved to keep away from them today. This would prove tricky since the wake was in the afternoon, but she didn't have to talk to them before or during or maybe ever again if that suited them. She sighed. That was hateful, just plain hateful, no two ways around it. It hurt anytime she felt guilty of being as bad as she judged them to be. She squeezed her eyes even tighter closed and asked God for forgiveness. Even so, she wanted to spend the day away from them; for that, she didn't feel ashamed. Some quality Edy time would do her good.

She still planned on calling the funeral home to verify all the arrangements were in order…and the minister…and the cemetery. Also, she had to call home and appoint a new botanical and veterinary caretaker. Plus, she needed to have a heart to heart with Ruth and apologize for her snippiness the day before. Such a busy day—*Lord, give me strength*—she turned, considering briefly just staying in bed, then reached a hand out from under the covers to peek through the curtain. *Hmm.* Looked like another grey day was in store. Had she slipped into an alternate universe where there was no sun and light simply reflected from her depressive spirit and colored the sky with gloom?

"Alright, Edy, that's enough. Time for coffee."

She rounded the doorway into Ruth's room, wearing a

mock sorry look on her face. Ruth was already dressed and swiping on her phone. Despite her eyes being locked onto the screen, she sensed her friend's presence.

"Let me guess, you don't know why you came, you give give give and they take take take, and you're sorry for being stressed out to the point of getting terse with innocent bystanders." Ruth looked up. "Does that about cover it?"

Edy's face froze for a moment before she answered, "Still. I'm sorry."

Ruth's eyebrows jumped as she started walking toward the door.

"Coffee?" was all she said.

A smile answered the question, and Edy followed. Her best friend made it too easy sometimes, and the grace with which she did it was right after the example of the Master. How could Ruth show anything else to a woman who gave so much to her family her whole life, and then continued to do so once she started her own family? All for the least amount of appreciation as they could possibly show. That was the magic of their friendship, and any good friendship: mutual respect. Edy saw Ruth as a saint for her compassion and Christlike love, and Ruth saw Edy's selflessness as mirroring the Lord's own character.

After coffee and breakfast, Edy went out for a walk. She had no idea how long she would be gone. This time, Ruth didn't offer to go with her. She knew Edy was in a place where she could finally sort some thoughts out and decided to give Nancy some pointers on her garden and landscape. Edy was happy to get out and revisit the neighborhood when it wasn't pouring down rain…which it might do at any time, the way her luck had been lately.

She had her phone with her, of course, but she was going to ignore all calls and texts from her siblings. Her original plan had been to sit at Nancy's and mope all day until the wake, but she knew they would just come and beat the woman's door down looking for her. So, she set out on foot, sneaking out the back door so none of them would see her leave, cutting through the rear neighbor's open yard to the next street. So far, no one had tried to contact her. *Hmm. No big deal. It's still early.* Not that she cared.

She was reminded of being a teenager years ago, when her mom and dad would go out of town. Being the oldest, she was left in charge. It never took long after their departure for her siblings to begin defying her. If their taking her for granted got too bad, she would have to pull back and almost withdraw completely. Meals, transportation, laundry...eventually they would figure out that they did, in fact, need her.

Edy called home to check in on everything. John said the flowers looked fine, though he only looked at them from the kitchen window. When she asked him about the watering, his response may as well have been 'Am I my brother's keeper?' for all its smug pretense. Harry was going to take over the gardening duties, despite Edy's prohibition. All he had to do was water, but with his testudineous mobility, it would take him all day. She asked why John had flaked on his responsibility, and he said it was because he was taking care of the cat.

"Put your dad on."

Harry, the weakened specter, came on the phone, agitated from his dormant state but always pleased by the sound of Edy's voice. He asked how everything was going in his minimalistic way of talking.

"Oh, they're just awful, of course."

It was a rare instance in which Edy Baldy still leaned on her husband for spousal support, having no one else to turn to.

A barely audible 'yeah' was mumbled, but with what feeling he could muster. Telling her the flowers looked good was his best attempt at encouragement. Edy didn't know why but she suddenly thought of Harry as he used to be, long ago, when she first fell for him. He was just a more energetic version of what he was today, but it was the distance between the two Harrys, and the distance to her that filled her with melancholy. Harry kept talking and Edy nodded verbally, neither knowing who was leading the conversation, like an awkward high school dance. It didn't matter because she wasn't really invested. The distance, the separation between her and her siblings was chasmic. She had always felt separate from them, like they had grown up in two different houses. Like they were family, and she was more a trusted neighbor, granted a limited access to the inner circle but not blood. Even their names bore witness to it. Edith? Edith Wilhelmina? Who in this century would be called Edith Wilhelmina? Her, that's who. For crying out loud, her maiden initials were EWW. Her siblings, on the other hand, had more contemporary names, names that said hip, up-and-comer, winner. They could have been the house band for a late-night talk show: Lenny and His Winning Wimmers.

She forgot she was still on the phone with Harry, so she told him to be careful and not overexert himself and she'd call him tomorrow. As she flipped her phone shut, she chuckled at the silly thought of her father as a big band leader. The Winning Wimmers. Maybe they'd periodically throw her a guest spot on kazoo. She felt a surprise pang of pity for her siblings. It wasn't really their fault; they had been raised different. The expectations for them were higher, and there were times in her youth when she could really feel the strain it put on them. Seeing them as the adult versions of those children, she almost cried. She wanted to go to them, but instantly stopped herself. She was tired of appearing weak to them.

"Forgive me, Lord."

Taking a deep breath, she decided to, instead of spending the day away in bitter resentment, spend it isolated from toxic influences to recenter herself on God and lean into Him for strength.

"Oh, Lord, I was so looking forward to this trip. I saw it as an opportunity for us all to come closer. I wanted to share You with them. I know it's a funeral, but I thought we could finally all feel loved and together like family, that the distance I've felt for so long would finally be closed. It hurts me so.

"Father, why don't I have the same lives they have? We came from the same house, the same upbringing, but they have…I just always felt that I was good enough to have it, too. I know Your will decided the path I would take long ago, and You are wise. I'm not unhappy, Lord, I just… forgive me for my envy. Help me to honor You, O God. Amen."

Sneaking back into Nancy's yard, Edy passed Ruth and their host inspecting her elephant ears. *Looks like mealybugs*, Edy didn't even hear herself thinking it. She went inside to her room and sat down to read Scripture.

There was a nagging emptiness clawing at the back of her consciousness. It's always been there, she knew, but she had never figured it out. She had always told herself that not knowing gave her something to dig into someday when she had spare time, like organizing a junk drawer or tackling a jigsaw puzzle. She knew it related to her family, though, but at the moment she was fed up with them, so she pushed the nag out of her thoughts. *Some other day, jigsaw.* As she read from God's Word, she felt the familiar hug of the Lord's love around her spirit that always made her think of Psalm 119:50. *This is my comfort in my affliction, that Your Word has revived me.* As she thought about the comfort she drew from the Bible, in perfect fashion her mind wanted to drift away from it, like Peter having already felt the water firmly underfoot and then, being scared by the wind, began to sink away from Christ's surety. It was almost compulsory, she thought about everything that worried her on a regular basis. She thought about home, about Harry, about John, about Geoffrey, about Duke Archibald, and, of course, the lilies.

She stopped herself right there. Her temples hurt, and her brow was damp. *That's enough.* She suddenly missed the calming effect of Scripture from just a moment ago, felt the distance between her and it, and realized what a nuisance anxiety was. She knew it was God's desire that she should draw closer to Him and be enriched by His testimony to man. Everything else was just…

"Distraction."

She opened her eyes, not knowing she had closed them.

Oh, but how did *things get this bad between us?*

She looked up from the Book to the window, her heart

bounding to them through the walls. Like Samuel and King Saul, the distance was short but strong. She stared at the house for a moment, watched as silhouettes moved across the curtains, no longer suspecting them of plotting and scheming against her. Her mind traveled back in time many years. It was Christmas. Perry Como's voice floated from the record player and sweetly flavored the air in the house. The tree was trimmed, decorated, and oh, so beautifully lit. Her parents always loved Christmas; they went all out. Edy remembered how she was just enchanted by the Christmas season even from an early age. Everything about it captured her heart: the decorations, the general atmosphere, the togetherness, the way it brought out the absolute best in humanity. She never saw anything beyond it, though. When December finally arrived each year, the world shut down in her mind and became consumed by Rudolph and nativity scenes and cookies and carols. Her siblings, however, even in childhood, had different focuses. Thoughts about direction in life, how everything correlated with their goals. It floored Edy now to see them back then, thinking about such adult things. She was in her early twenties, yet it felt like they were all older than her. She heard the music, and it was one of the building blocks of her holiday spirit, whereas it was merely a brief diversion for the rest of them. And through it all, she realized, her father guided them in this thinking, all the while letting little Edith Wimmer enjoy all the pretty colors and merriment. She looked hard at the scene before her, watched herself sort of fade into the background, almost as an afterthought, while Dad gave close attention—even eye contact—to everyone else.

It was at that moment that Edith Wilhelmina Baldy

realized that through her entire life it wasn't their things that she envied. It wasn't really even envy, she knew, that plagued her. She didn't want their money, their cars, houses, or friends. It wasn't their successes. It was their father's approval. That was all she ever wanted. She realized she had always associated their success with the approval they got from Dad. They had it, and she didn't. She heard that she shouldn't seek anyone's acceptance but Christ's, but even He drew a parallel between divine and earthly fatherhood. There was no sin in wanting to know her daddy loved her. They took it for granted and didn't even know they had it, but to Edy it was more valuable than gold. She let the tears flow freely—how many more could she possibly have in her—and thanked God for all He had shown her. She casually noticed rain drops on the window multiplying. For a brief moment, she found it beautiful.

A knock on the door brought her away from it. Ruth announced herself, and Edy called her in. It was almost time to leave for the wake, she knew. Ruth was always good at reminders. Edy's smile ran off her face like excess paint down a canvas as she proceeded to tell her friend that she had arranged for the will reading to be done early the morning after the funeral so that they could leave immediately afterward. She was taking Dad's car back home. She still didn't want or need it, but to waffle now would only make her look more a fool to them than she already did. She didn't care about money or the estate, she just wanted out. Ruth, in typical Ruth fashion, gave Edy her support, but urged her not to leave things this way, bitter and full of resentment. She gently reminded her it was un-Christlike and left Edy to get changed.

Edy watched the door after it closed and stared hard. *Yes, yes, of course, Ruth.* Edy knew her friend was right, but she knew what she was doing. She wasn't going to leave them disgruntled, but she needed to leave them. There was nothing new to discuss, everything was as it ever was. She wondered if they would ever change. Contemplation took advantage of her state, and she reached for her phone. As she listened to the ringing, she just had to know how far the acorn fell from the tree.

"Hello?"

"Geoffrey, hi."

Geoffrey asked how everything was going, and Edy tripped over her words, frantic to get it out, but wanting to tread lightly.

"Geoffrey, I…I…"

"Mom?"

"I need to ask you something, I…"

"What is it, Mom?" The worry in his voice reached her.

"Honey, was I a good mother?"

The sound of laughter on the other end of the line did not soothe Edy's worry.

"I'm being serious, Geoffrey."

"Sorry, Mom, I just…you caught me off guard."

A pause.

"Well?"

"They must have really worked you into a tizzy this time."

"Are you going to answer the question or not?"

"Mom, you were and still ARE a GREAT mother."

There was silence, so he knew she was crying.

"Mom, what's wrong?"

She composed herself enough to speak.

"Nothing, son. Thank you. I have to go to a wake now."

"Aren't you going to ask me how I'm doing, Supermom?"

"Oh, my goodness, I'm so sorry, yes, I…"

"I'm kidding, Mom. Go. I love you."

"I love you, too, Geoffrey. Goodbye."

She hung up and clenched her phone tightly with both hands, sobbing as quietly as she could. Ruth stood on the other side of the door, her own eyes no longer dry.

"God bless that boy," she whispered before moving on.

The wake, which Edy found out last minute was being held in her father's house, was a typical affair. The rain had stopped, and the clouds that brought it were all gone. The sky was almost white, though, and Edy knew the sun was just on the other side of that empyrean sheet, mighty but holding back from penetrating the overcast. There was an electricity to it, and under different circumstances she would draw from its energy a verve that would make her mood hum all day. But this was a wake, and that verve was stuck between the solemnity of the occasion and the tension between the surviving Wimmers. The expanse looked superimposed over the house and the street and the somberly dressed people walking up to the door. It was juxtaposition at its suburban finest.

Edy entered the house invisibly as usual. Ignoring six people would be difficult in a house this size, but their rigid postures seemed to say they were willing to support the cause. Edy studied each one briefly before looking at whoever they were talking to. She recognized a few faces, but there were more she didn't. Thomas was talking to Mr. Sandersen, Dad's old golf buddy, whose hardness of hearing was making Thomas visibly uncomfortable. Poor Nancy was cornered by Stuart, who Edy always suspected had a bit of a crush on the woman, a theory that was at least corroborated by Claudia's disapproving glance. Wesley was pretending to enjoy his conversation with Buckley Qualls, a car salesman that Dad had mentored from day one. "Buck" was ten years Dad's junior, and it was said the latter took a shine to the former because he, too, was a veteran. He had always looked up to Leonard Wimmer and was truly grieved by his passing. Edy smiled because that was the genuine sentiment that she wanted the house to be filled with right now.

It was a typical affair for the sort, people coming and going, subdued socializing, light refreshments. Edy couldn't help but try puzzling out whose idea it was to do it here. It was surely cheaper this way...who was the cheapskate of the bunch? *Stop it, Edy. This is not the place.* Still, it did hurt whenever she saw them talking with each other but not her... despite the fact that she resolutely did not wish to speak with any of them. It felt really hot in the house, but Caroline was blocking the thermostat, so Edy positioned herself close to a floor vent to catch what pitiful relief it could offer. Ruth was careful not to stand too close, but never left her alone. It was also very dark. For as bright as the sky was, all the blinds were down and closed, and there was only one pale lamp lit in the main room. *Cave bats.* She grinned but dropped it immediately. *Eeedyyy.* Still, where were the hooded monks? Did the dirges start after hors d'oeuvres? She had half a mind to go back to Nancy's and pick out something more colorful to wear. Something outrageous. Well, Edy Baldy didn't really own anything outrageous, but she wished she did at that moment. Geoffrey's wife, Amy, owned some things that she thought were outrageous, and had most likely commented on them at some point, probably to Ruth even. She wished Amy were with her just now, wearing her most outrageous outfit. She really was a sweet girl, and Edy loved her very much. She loved her departed father, too. He may not have been perfect, but he was her father and he deserved better than this dismal affair. *They* certainly had plenty to honor him for.

When everyone had left, and it was just the Wimmers—plus Ruth—Edy was approached by the collective. They offered a pathetic attempt at an apology that would have probably passed when they were teenagers, but now was as easy to see through as a freshly cleaned window. Uncharacteristic of Edy, she held her ground and scoffed at the façade. They weren't sorry about anything, she knew, and she was done pretending. It never paid off, and besides, she was the only one making believe. Their deluded reality and Edy's grasp at fantasy resulted in an incompatibility for resolution. Maybe they truly were hopeless, but that was always the moment when Edy brought herself back to the reality she knew. Nobody was beyond hope with God still on the throne.

The siblings then accused Edy of being "un-Christian" for calling their bluff. She fumed at this, her pet peeve, people who never mentioned God except to accuse someone else of falling short of His glory. Tensions were high, having never subsided any since their big argument. Ruth quickly stepped in and pulled Edy away, staring daggers at the Wimmers. She enjoyed the unique advantage of being an outsider, not having to be afraid if any of them never wanted to see her again. As they made it outside, Edy noticed a finely-dressed man standing next to a rented Porsche, blocking the driveway. She had been so sad not to see him when she first arrived, and now he was here. She knew Henry would probably always be a baby in her eyes.

"What took you so long?" she huffed angrily at him as she walked on past to cross the street.

Though none of them went as far as to go knock on Nancy's door, they each took a turn trying to get Edy on the phone throughout the rest of that day. She told them all the same thing: to leave a message after the tone.

10

"SOLES ON THE JORDAN"

(JOSH. 1:2-3)

Morning rose to Edy's presence by the bedside, solemn and resolute. No internal dialogue to disturb the silence of the dark that filled her room. Today was about her father, she knew. Nothing else mattered. As sometimes in life certain situations bring a temporary truce between a person and their adversaries, so this moment found Edith Wilhelmina Baldy with her back to all her surrounding interference. She knew, though, that she had not conquered any mountains; she still could not see the other side, but the hulking mass temporarily did not blind her from knowing the other side was there. Also, the weather forecast was optimistic. An overcast sky would give way to clear blue for a brief window.—Pretty much right during the funeral. She wasn't shaken, though. To let her eyes be burned by the sun's rays even for a moment would be welcome after such a long absence.

Edy spent the morning in seclusion. Bordering on

dramatic, it was a total departure from character. Yet, no knock came upon her door, no ring from her phone. She did not emerge until it was time to leave, and when she did it was with the utmost propriety. A respectful maroon top, accented with black around the edges, and black pants, she looked quite lovely. The personal touch was the brooch fastened to her left lapel. It had belonged to her mother and was her father's favorite piece of her jewelry. Nancy complimented the ensemble before insisting she drive them.

Everspring Funeral Chapel stood beautifully against the backdrop of the morning. True to the weatherman's prediction, the sky was looking favorable for an appearance by the sun, and Edy's sorrow was distracted by her hopefulness to see it. Inside, she went around the room reserved for her family, making sure all the arrangements were in order. Some beautiful floral bouquets had been delivered. She still couldn't believe Henry waited to the last minute to come, but he had always kept a distance from them. She was almost jealous of the tactic. Her nose reacted to an obvious dust surplus, but she did her best to ignore it. Soothing guitar music played softly above her head as she made her way to the front. This was a surreal moment for Edy. She hadn't seen her father's face in several months, and now it was just there, lifeless but painted to look lifelike. It was the final step in making the whole thing real to her. He was actually gone, no more room for denial, not that she had been struggling with any. She gazed upon him for a moment before moving on, heading to the rear of the chapel. She wondered how faux pas it would be for her to attend the ceremony seated there. Oh, but it would drive *them* nuts. *No no. Focus on Dad.*

As people began filing in, Edy knew she should move up front to her proper place. Yet, she remained sitting, Bible in her lap and a searing focus in her eyes. She didn't even know what she was thinking, or what she was looking so intently at, but she didn't budge. A crackling, hissing, electrical noise burned inside her ears, and she bled her stresses out through its frequency. All the things in life that worried her, she focused on their positives. Her flowers were so pretty, and she loved tending to them. She loved watching the sun kiss their leaves in the mid-morning as it rose higher in a clear sky. They would sway so softly in a summer breeze, in a hypnotic floating dance that Edy felt she could watch for hours. Sometimes, when a wind picked up while she was watering, a drop or two would blow away and land on her foot. It was odd, she knew, but she would feel a kinship with the lilies in those moments. When she was younger and just started dating Harry, her hair was long and laid on her shoulders, so complaisantly at ease. Even when disturbed by a gust, it was lovely and composed. As a child, one of John's favorite things in the fall was after Harry had finished raking all the leaves and went off to get some bags and a strong western blow would kick up and ruin the pile, he would shriek with laughter and chase the leaves further away. And her siblings...

"As for man, his days are like grass; as a flower of the field, so he flourishes."

Edy hadn't even noticed the minister coming up, but the passage from Psalm 103 was a familiar one and it called her to focus as he continued.

"When the wind has passed over it, it is no more, and its place acknowledges it no longer."

She took a deep breath and felt at ease. She felt relaxed. Edith Wilhelmina Baldy felt relaxed at a funeral. She was the picture of tranquility, and she hoped a smile wasn't creeping up on her face. She looked around at all the attendees. Mrs. Lazenby, who knew Dad from the church he rarely attended, was casually consoling her face with a wadded tissue. She was a sweet lady; Edy knew it was genuine. So many folks looking sad and somber—and all they had to do was put on black and drive out. She had endured so much to be here, but then she paused, reminding herself that this moment was not about her. It was perfect. He deserved this exact mood. Respect and silent admiration, he would be pleased and, therefore, so was she. Suddenly, she realized Ruth was sitting next to her, on her right. Of course she was. She didn't look to Ruth's face, and she hadn't sensed her presence per se. A stiff side glance at the dress…yep it was her. An abrupt swelling in the light, a hue of shadow changed, and Edy knew it was out. She had but to turn her head and surely she would see its golden rays touching the world outside. So why was her neck not spinning like a top? She would be able to see its light, but she wouldn't have its warmth upon her skin. Its physical presence alone, she knew, was not what she desired. She wanted the heat, the blinding light, she wanted to watch it grow things taller. Just knowing the sun was out did nothing for her. She wanted to experience it. Edy jerked her attention back to the minister standing at the front of the assembly. He was clutching the sides of the podium and his head was bowed. He was praying. Edy stared at him, and suddenly it clicked that she should bow her head as well.

"Amen."

She hadn't caught a word of the eulogy. It was a beautiful service.

People began to leave, and one older woman walked right past Edy and said, "I didn't see the oldest girl here. Is she still living?"

Edy couldn't resist a grin, especially since she had no idea who the woman was. Looking up at her siblings, her grin vanished, and she noticed they all seemed to have a nervous tension about them, like they were desperately scanning the room for something to do. Edy approached them with an austere steeliness. Without announcing herself or clearing her throat or some such thing, she just started talking.

"I wanted this occasion to bring us closer. I thought maybe things had been mended, but I realize now that was foolish of me. To think that losing Dad would magically heal our relationship was a really bad case of wishful thinking. It's just left us angry...er, angrier. Anyway, the will's being read tomorrow, and I don't care if Dad didn't leave me a penny. I'm leaving immediately afterward."

She paused.

"All I've ever wanted was what you all had."

They all assumed she was talking about money.

"I wanted Dad to care about me like he did you. I wanted him to worry about me like he did you. I wanted him to look at me like he did you. But he didn't, and now it doesn't matter. Except it does, because otherwise I wouldn't be saying anything."

Here came the tears. *No, no. Don't let them see it.*

"You are all so hurtful to me, and maybe it's not even your fault. But...hurtful, nonetheless. Still," she looked down at her shoes to try to compose herself, "you're my family, and I love you. I'll always love you."

And that was it. She hadn't intended to say that much, and she knew it wasn't really the appropriate setting for such an address. Indeed, Ruth's face was a bit stiff, like she wanted to say something halfway through that speech but resisted because she knew it needed to be said. And because she didn't want things to escalate. With that, Edy left the chapel, and Ruth followed promptly behind. As usual, none of the siblings budged.

The following day, Edy and Ruth were all packed and ready to go. Edy felt absolutely dreadful, as in ill, for multiple reasons. A cavalcade of emotions had come to a head and were now desperate to be flushed out. She hugged Nancy warmly, downcast to be leaving her uplifting company. She wanted to whisper *why couldn't you be my sister?* into the woman's ear, but she knew there really was no point. She had been a blessing to Edy, but the time had come for them to part, and it hurt her physically to be turning the page. When her hostess said, "Come back anytime," Edy was completely useless in holding back the tears. What twisted her stomach into so many more knots, though, was knowing where she was headed before going home. This was like the real goodbye, not just to her father, but to her actual sister and brothers. She was so disappointed in them and so desperate to be accepted by them.

Humid air was heavy around the car as they drove through it like cattle lumbering lazily out of the way. The sky was bright, but the sun was still blocked by thin clouds; Edy, for all her bitterness, was still longing to see the sun like a fish out of water. It was the most central element of her outdoorsy green thumb personality, and she felt pangs in her spirit from its prolonged absence. She wasn't angry at God; she knew she didn't know His mind—couldn't know His mind. At no point was her frustration directed at her heavenly Father, she just understood that everything was under His supervision and control, every turn of the road part of His divine decree. She just wished she could understand how it all fit into His plan.

They drove in silence to the attorney's office, Ruth at the helm and Edy an antiquated picture of dignity. Two hands on the purse in her lap, stiff back, and chin up, her determined posture was very transparent. Only her jaw moved, almost unnoticeably, to work out her anxiety into a rhythm. She didn't want her father's car anymore. She never wanted it to begin with, but certainly not now. The very idea of it left a very unpleasant taste in her mouth. She didn't want to be like them. She *wasn't* like them. It had rained overnight. She was afraid to call home, sure that the flowers had been ravaged by wild locusts. *Only three more days* she thought. Three more days until the ribbon was awarded. She would make it just in time.

Ruth pulled in front of the building to drop Edy off.

"I'll wait for you. Edy," she paused, "everything will be alright."

Edy smiled and closed the door. Entering the suite, the secretary told Edy to go on back and that all her siblings were already there. Of course they were. This was the day they had all been waiting for; time to divvy up Dad's stuff. Well, maybe not Henry. He didn't need a dime of Dad's money and had no interest in any of his stuff; probably the biggest reason he hadn't shown up until the last minute.

As she entered the office, the mood was tense, but it was a different kind of tension. Up till now it had always been an awkward tension, the siblings all feeling sheepish toward their oldest sister. Now, though, the feeling was changed, like they were unabashed about their behavior. Why not? It no longer mattered. Edy had always known how they felt, and now they knew how she felt. It was understood that this may very well be the last time they would see her, and that that was okay with them. None of them looked at her, nor she at them. The lawyer was clearly untouched by the foulness, no doubt he had become immune to it throughout the course of his practice. He wasted no time in getting down to business.

The business, though, was very brief. In a turn of events that no one saw coming but were left to compute with their jaws resting on the floor, Edy inherited everything. Everything. Leonard Wimmer had left his entire estate to his eldest child, Edith Wilhelmina Baldy. All his worldly goods, his money, his house, and even his car went to her. The lawyer did a commendable job of conveying his client's emotions to his primary heir as he read a statement from the deceased. He had watched her step into the role left vacant by her mother's passing without flinching, like a switch came on when his wife died. There was no question, she just knew what to do. He knew she could handle the responsibility of overseeing everything with honesty and fairness. He had always known her qualities, and they were the ones he loved most in her mother. Had a pin dropped at that moment, despite the fact that the floor was carpeted, it would have sounded like a window breaking. Everyone's best efforts to hide their feelings were flimsy. Their shock was too great.

Trying hard not to love every bit of it, Edy stood, the picture of poise and grace, and thanked the attorney. Turning to leave, without making eye contact, she told Wesley to kindly give her the key to her new summer home. The architect was so stunned, and not knowing what words he could possibly say, he handed her the key. She left with a confident gait, unable to resist turning up her nose.

She walked out of the office and her pace quickened with each step out to the car. The sky was so grey now, but Edy hardly noticed it as she jumped into the car. The worry was heavy on Ruth's face, and she opened her mouth to speak.

"Just drive, please, dear," came Edy first.

As they pulled out of the parking lot, she just burst into laughter as tears gushed out of her face. It was over. The weight of this experience was too much, and Edy knew she couldn't carry it anymore and she could've never carried it alone. She was so thankful for Ruth's presence and her friendship. Then she thought about her father. Her entire life she had sought his approval, only to discover she'd had it all along. She sobbed and sobbed and thanked Jesus and sobbed. It was messy and awkward, and Ruth didn't say a word. This was her dearest friend bleeding out from her heart, a pain she'd kept far too long. She cried right along with her, silently, with her eyes fixed on the road.

The car rolled into the driveway of the dearly departed Wimmer and came to a jostled halt at Ruth's classic brake punch. Edy had never been fond of her friend's driving, but it was something that she had been able to just ignore with ease for all the years she'd known her. She got out of the car, still the picture of perfectly composed dignity, and went into the house. A moment later, the garage door opened, faster than usual, almost like it wanted to clear out of Edy's way. Then the car that Edy had fought for without really wanting backed out slowly. Very slowly. Ruth had always felt Edy's driving was so conservative it would annoy the most rigid driving instructor, and she was not so shy in bringing it up from time to time. She was almost completely out when she noticed Wesley shuffling nervously up alongside the car. She lowered the window with a perfect smirk on her face, knowing what he was going to say. Or rather, what he wanted to say. All that came out was a pitiful babbling stammer, a quick pause, and then an "Is this what Dad would want?" that was almost painful to watch.

The corners of Edy's mouth budged almost unnoticeably before she spoke.

"Please, dear Wesley. I have an award to accept."

And the car kept moving. The garage door began to come down, and as Edy positioned the car homeward, she looked across the street to see Nancy in her window, with the biggest smile her face could handle beaming back at her. Edy returned the sentiment and drove off, Ruth following close behind.

Edy chuckled to herself. They had only sent Wesley.

"I would've brought everyone," she said aloud. "It wouldn't have worked...but I would've brought them all."

They still just didn't get it. *The ignorance that is in them, because of the hardness of their heart. Boy, you said it, Paul.* Then Edy breathed a heavy sigh. She didn't mean it hatefully. She didn't mean any of it hatefully, and she knew God knew it, too. She truly didn't care about any of the stuff. She knew she would do exactly what her father trusted her to do, oversee the distribution of the estate. *But let them squirm a bit.* She couldn't stop the grin.

After an hour on the road, Edy's head was still buzzing. There was so much work to be done. She would have to return in the near future, but most of the work could be done by her siblings, who were now, no doubt, somewhat fearful of their eldest sister, or at least her upper hand. The sky was still unrelenting in its captivity of the sun, but the light was trying to break through. It was a type of overcast that always forced Edy to put her sunglasses on, otherwise she would get a headache, and she didn't need another one. She sighed again. For just a brief moment, she had peace. She knew she would see the sun again. Everything would settle. She knew her siblings weren't evil. They were human, just like her, and eventually they would properly mourn the loss of their father, each in their own way. For now, though, there was a house to sell, finances to settle, possessions to go through, and, of course, a car to purchase. Now that she had her siblings' attention, she knew she would get some cooperation from them. Still, she hoped that God would work through the situation to bring them all closer. She gripped the wheel and prayed.

Edy soon realized the biggest drawback to her and Ruth being in two separate cars was that she no longer had someone to talk to. She knew she wasn't above talking to herself, but she didn't have Ruth's wit, and she didn't want the conversation she had with herself to be a flat one. She looked southward with a sadness in her eyes that was just begging the sun to appear, a sadness born from accepting a world without sunshine. It had become normal to her to see grey, only grey. She took a deep breath, ignoring the sky as one ignores a pet they love dearly that just knocked over a vase of flowers. Maybe some alone time would be good for them both. It would give Edy a chance to reflect on everything without risk of any interruptions. Plus, she could play all her Herb Alpert albums she loved so much—and Ruth couldn't stand. Edy paused. She took a moment to richly savor the gift from God that Ruth was. She had been a rock for Edy this entire trip, even in times when she said nothing at all. It was a blessed friendship that, sadly, not every person born is fortunate enough to know. She thought of David and Jonathan and a smile, warm like a womb, spread over her face.

As dinner time approached, Ruth suddenly pulled around Edy and took the lead. Edy followed, of course, when Ruth disembarked the interstate. She drove a few minutes into town and pulled into a restaurant parking lot. As they faced each other for the first time since they set out, it was like a reunion with a long-lost friend. They hadn't been apart this long since leaving Mureau Heights. It was very refreshing for Edy, so it was only fitting for her to comment on how far off the highway the restaurant was. Ruth was never one to hide annoyance.

"How did you even know about this place?" Edy asked.

"I've been researching eateries on our route for a few days, hoping to avoid another Farmer's Wife incident."

Edy took the remark personally and stiffened her neck to repel it. She still felt bad about that whole deal. She had considered returning on their way home. Not as a patron, of course, but to confront them on their obviously low sanitation standards. She knew, however, that it would accomplish nothing, and she would just come off all wrong.

They wouldn't care. She prayed instead that God would bring about a reform for their establishment.

As she sat down, she realized she hadn't even paid attention to what the restaurant she just entered was called. It didn't matter. In a rare moment for her, she was just happy to be paused from the whole scene, to be back in her friend's company, and to be having a meal. Ruth told her she had already booked them a hotel for the night, making sure to add "about an hour ago."

Now it was Edy's turn to be annoyed, and she chided Ruth for using her phone while driving.

"You don't even own a smartphone, Edith. How do you know how dangerous it is?"

"Well, *I* don't use *any* kind of phone while I'm driving."

It was said as though Ruth was hearing it for the first time.

Ruth picked up a menu and locked eyes on it.

"How are you doing, deary?"

The tone suggested she had been worrying the whole time on the road. Edy was looking at her flip phone.

"Sixteen missed calls. All from my siblings."

"Are you going to call them back?"

"Nope," Edy answered as punctuation to snapping her phone shut.

"Attagirl," said Ruth, still not looking up.

"I'm sure they're all stammering from the shock of me actually leaving. Probably had a few bucks between them on whether I'd turn back."

The two ladies laughed as the waiter came over to the table. After he left with an order for two iced teas, Edy got serious.

"Ruth?"

Ruth fixed her eyes back on the menu and answered the obvious with, "I know, Edy. It's okay."

"Still," Edy started to get teary, which she knew was why Ruth wouldn't look at her, "it means a lot to me. God bless you."

Ruth squinted and asked the rafters if the broiled flounder was any good.

The next morning, Edy awoke feeling positive and refreshed. She had dreamed about being in her garden at home, soaked in sunshine. She realized the further she got from what was behind her, the closer she got to her flowers, which, according to the reports, had been getting plenty of sun. Later that day, while driving, Edy's phone began to ring. She picked it up without thinking and saw it was Geoffrey calling. She briefly considered taking the call. *I can be hip like Ruth.* She declined, though, as her cautious side took over and she concluded that whatever he wanted could wait until they stopped for lunch. Suddenly, her mind began to fill with thoughts of her siblings and what machinations they were devising. Maybe she shouldn't have left it like that. Maybe she should have told them she wasn't going to keep everything. Wesley *had* to know she was kidding about the 'summer house' thing. Didn't he? What if they were all cleaning out the house at that very moment? Calling their respective lawyers to find out what could be done to contest the will, refuting Dad's specific wishes. They didn't need to do it, she anxiously thought. She was just kidding. NO! She loosened her grip on the steering wheel and calmed herself. So what if they were doing all those things. She had the car. *I can't believe I took the car.* She didn't care about any of that other stuff. Let them do what they wished. She drove on, positive attitude reinstated.

In fact, she felt so positive, she decided to live dangerously and call Geoffrey back. Now. While driving. Edith Wilhelmina Baldy was going to make a phone call while driving. She was almost giddy from the excitement of the idea. Plus, she was happy at the thought of speaking to him. She couldn't wait to tell him what she was doing while talking to him.

"Mom?"

His tone was not good, and Edy's face dropped.

"Geoffrey?" was her worried response.

"Mom…I'm so sorry………"

Edy brought the car to a screeching halt on the shoulder of the interstate as the raindrops began their dance on her windshield.

11

"OVERCOME"

(JOHN 16:33)

Ruth's reflexes weren't quick enough, and she pulled over ahead of Edy before stopping. When she came up to the passenger side of the late Wimmer's car, through the rain she saw her friend breaking down with her phone pressed up to her ear. *Edy never uses the phone while driving.* Edy was frantic and hurriedly lowered the window.

"Edy, put the window up and unlock the door, it's pouring!" Ruth shouted over her friend's sobs and the loud rain. She was concerned, but she was also getting wet quickly.

When the door clicked, Ruth threw it open and shut behind her, and set to the task of calming Edy. She had only ever seen her like this once or twice before, and it scared her.

Edy was still holding the phone to her ear, and Ruth wondered silently if there was still anybody on the other end. She gently coaxed Edy to give it to her and put it on speaker. Poor Geoffrey had to explain everything a second time. A bad storm had flared up during the night, and a tree in her next-door neighbor's yard split almost in two. Fortunately, Edy's house was untouched, but she almost didn't care. Hours on her knees caring for her lilies was now all gone, nothing to show. The neighbor, Mr. Ashley, was just beside himself with grief over it. He had always gotten along well with the Baldys and knew how much the flowers meant to Edy.

Ruth continued to talk with Geoffrey for a moment. Edy stopped listening as she wept. Everything was ruined. All that hard work, this was *her* year, she'd been sure of it. She was still a day away from even being able to see the wreckage. Suddenly, all the moments from the last few days she had told herself she didn't even care about the flowers anymore came rushing back to her at once. But the truth was that the garden and her confidence that she would win the competition were the things that were always there in her heart, sure and certain. It was that "at least I've got…" comfort waiting for her when she got back home. She noticed her phone lit up and she looked at the screen. Thomas was calling, and Edy rolled her eyes. She didn't see Ruth look up at her to see her reaction. She suddenly felt like Israel fleeing Egypt. She feared that if she looked in her mirror at that moment, she would see her siblings all following her, gaining on her in some sort of post-apocalyptic band of marauders formation. It was ridiculous, she knew, and she stopped herself there. She took a deep breath. This hurt, but God was still on the throne, still in control.

"Geoffrey."

Edy had spoken right in the middle of the conversation, but she either didn't know or didn't care. Her tone was authoritative and her face resolute. Ruth looked at her, uncertain what this was.

"Geoffrey, we're on our way home. We'll be there tomorrow afternoon."

"Mom?" came his meek reply.

"Everything's going to be okay, son. We need to get off the shoulder, it's pouring down rain right now."

Ruth didn't know what to think. Suddenly Edy was comforting Geoffrey? This was strange, but she knew rolling with it was her best bet.

"Okay, Mom, jus…just be safe…and I'll see you when you get here. I'm so sorry, Mom."

Edy hung up the phone, staring straight ahead at the highway before them. The mission was getting home. The competition was over. For her, at least. She looked over at Ruth, who had a very un-Ruth-like look on her face. The curve ball of Edy's assertiveness had really left her dumbfounded, but her instinct told her not to push. She knew her friend was right; the smartest thing to do was to get back on the road. It was strange for Edy to be right about such a thing during a time like this. So, she got out and trotted back to the Baldymobile, and waited for Edy to pull out. She wasn't quite white-knuckled, but she was unsure about Edy being alone behind the wheel right now. They really didn't have a choice, though, so she just followed at a distance that still allowed her to watch Edy's mannerisms. After a few miles, to Ruth's surprise, Edy's driving was pretty normal.—For Edy.

Edy *was* upset, though. She was grieving. She had just lost her father, and her siblings—her father's *other* children—weren't offering the support she had hoped for.

And she'd worked so hard to bring these flowers to blue ribbon worthiness. This was supposed to be *her* year.

The rain started picking up, getting heavier and louder. Ruth tightened her grip on the worn steering wheel while praying softly for her friend's safety.

Edy wanted the win so bad. She did the work—she should get the prize. She really was dealing with her father's death well. And suddenly she felt ashamed. Was that the only reason she had been able to keep it together? Because of her certainty that she would win Best Blossoms? Were her lilies a bigger deal than her father's passing?

Ruth watched Edy pulling away from her. *Oh, no, Edy, what are you doing?* She contemplated calling her, but now was not the time to divide Edy's focus. Or her own.

Edy began to pray out loud, open-eyed, of course. "Oh, Lord. I've always put my faith in You. I've always been content with what You've given me. I've never asked You to move any mountains for me. I've prayed for my family, prayed that You would keep them, that they would know You. I've always loved them—still do—despite how mean they are to me. And You're so good to me, and I love You."

Despite the rain, Ruth closed the distance between her and Edy just a little. She knew her friend was crying.

"I really wanted this, Lord." Edy's tears were flowing, but her focus was sharp. "My flowers were so pretty. They were good enough for Best Blossoms. They were good enough..." She banged on the wheel while her face throbbed. "I was good enough...I just wanted the recognition!...For someone to tell me I was good enough."

Ruth changed lanes to pull up alongside Edy. Something was wrong; Edy began slowing down. Edy didn't even notice the Baldymobile next to her, but Ruth was starting to feel frantic, fearing an accident any second. It was uncharacteristic of her, but she loved Edy and she knew the weight that her friend was carrying. "Oh, Lord Jesus, protect her, please."

"You took my father, and now You've taken my flowers, and I trust You…but I'm angry! I'm hurt! And am I EVER GOING TO SEE THE SUN AGAIN?!" Edy jerked the car to the shoulder yet again and came to an abrupt stop. She got out into the pouring rain and screamed. Screamed! SCREEEAMED!!!

Ruth pulled in behind her and hesitated to get out. She didn't know what this was, and she really didn't want to be wet. She knew Edy needed her, though, so she put her flashers on and checked the mirror before jumping out. She ran to her friend, who fell into her arms crying. The two stood there for a moment, completely soaked, and the rain suddenly stopped. In the middle of nowhere, the abrupt silence was almost louder than the roar of the rain had been. The only sound was Edy's loud sobbing, broken briefly by a lone car passing quickly by.

Later, at their hotel for the evening, Ruth was a little grumpy. She had the sniffles and wore her hotel robe like a hospital patient, clutching a wad of tissues as she moved listlessly about the room. She could never be unloving towards Edith, but she was miffed about the unexpected discomfort. And the fact that her friend was completely fine.

Edy was quiet and contemplative and took Ruth's "abuse" with a blank smile. She took the liberty of ordering a pizza to the room, but after that she was distant. The roadside scene earlier took a lot out of her, but she gave it freely. It needed to happen, and she knew it. Even though she was quiet and far away, she was in rather a good mood. She felt…cleansed. She had purged herself of so much in an emotional release that was long overdue. The best part was that she had been honest with God. She always believed that Christ followers had to occasionally remind themselves that it was okay to be hurt by God and be upset with Him. One can't control what emotions they feel, only how they manage their emotions. It was only natural for Edy to be angry about something that angered her, but she had maintained her faith and reverence. Still, it was a draining experience, but Edith Wilhelmina Baldy didn't feel drained, more…transfused. As much as she had flushed out, she had been filled with a humming energy that forced new perspective and ideas on her. She wasn't brooding sulkily, she was relishing freedom from baggage. Ruth kept on intermittently sneezing and complaining, knowing she was being ignored.

In the morning, they embarked on the final leg of their journey. The sky was a dark grey, but it wasn't raining, nor was there any forecast for rain. Both cars gassed and snacks secured, the ladies looked back at the hotel as though it represented the whole ordeal. It was such a tangled mess of feelings, but it had attached itself to them. It felt a little strange for it to end, but they knew later that afternoon they would be back in Mureau Heights and the normal life that now seemed foreign would resume. For Ruth, at least, nothing really would be different. She had borne burdens with Edy before, so she would just walk a little closer to her friend down the road of life, which didn't bother her in the slightest.

Edy drove stoically. She couldn't not feel upset about

the flowers, but she had accepted the reality of the situation. Over breakfast, she had, just for a moment, entertained the idea that Geoffrey was playing a prank on her with his bad news call. She dismissed this thought, however, knowing that *he* knew what would happen when she caught up to him. No, the flowers were gone, and since she couldn't turn back time, she took advantage of the opportunity to familiarize herself with her new car. It was luxurious, and she felt the blessing. Save for the stereo playing low, she drove in relative silence. It was a safe, but altogether boring trip.

Six hours later, they finally pulled into Edy's driveway. They hadn't stopped for lunch; neither felt in the mood really. Neither had noticed the Mureau Heights city limits sign. Neither had paid any attention to the streets decorated for Best Blossoms as they were every year. There were thick clouds above, but holes in the patchwork showed ocean blue. Ruth parked next to Edy in the double driveway and walked over to her window.

"Do you want me to stay awhile?" she asked, looking down at the door panel.

"That's alright. I've got things to do." Edy didn't want to look at the flowers, but she knew she wanted to see them alone.

"Well, hurry up and take me home, then." Ruth threw her bags in the back seat and hopped in up front.

Edy noticed the blue spots in the sky as she backed out.

When she parked at Ruth's house, Edy asked absentmindedly if she needed help with anything.

"I just can't get rid of you, can I?"

Edy laughed.

"Call me later," Ruth quickly changed her tone.

She grabbed her things and sauntered up to the driver door, knowing this was the official end of the journey for her. But it was Edy who spoke.

"I'll never forget how much you helped me on this trip."

Ruth smiled warmly, "I'll send you a bill," and went inside.

When Edy returned home, it set in that the new car was at its new home. She wondered if any of the neighbors were ogling it through their windows. She turned off the engine and sat in the driveway for a moment. She couldn't put it off any longer. They were just flowers, no point in being in denial about it. She took a deep breath and got out of the car. The curtain in John's room pulled back an inch, as it always did anytime a car door closed, and then fell dismissively back into place. Edy never noticed it, and she was certainly too preoccupied now. God was so good to her and had always met all her needs. She always felt loved by Him, and she knew everything she ever needed for emotional fulfillment could be found in Him.

As she rounded the back corner of the house, she took in the sight from a distance and paused. It was bad, yes. Bless their hearts, Geoffrey and Mr. Ashley had done their best to remove the downed limbs from the area, as one would respectfully give dignity to a dead person right before their spouse saw them. She couldn't stop a chuckle in her throat. How had she missed that tree all these years? Probably because it provided some of the shade she enjoyed while laboring outdoors. It wasn't the healthiest, and perhaps subconsciously she had been aware of how it loomed somewhat ominously over her flowers. Edy moved in closer and stood at the edge of what used to be her garden. She scanned slowly and her eyes rested on one solitary lily that remained. It was missing two petals and a sepal, but it stood straight and tall. Edy stared at it, past it really. She saw all the hours spent on her achy knees tending this garden, giving these flowers everything imaginable to help them thrive and succeed. But she didn't reminisce bitterly. She saw it playing back in her memory with a sense of completeness. Regardless of how everything turned out, she had put her all into it. And the flowers had been beautiful. *She* knew they were perfect, even if no one else ever would. Plus, God knew, and He was who the book of Colossians instructed her to work for. He had blessed them and brought them up from the ground. Edy focused in on the lone survivor and observed its damage in detail. Suddenly, the flower was lit by the brilliant, blinding rays of the sun covering it in radiant gilt work. It touched everything around it, and Edy felt its warmth on her back, simultaneously as something new and something familiar. Maybe next year would be her year. Without looking up, Edith Wilhelmina Baldy closed her eyes and smiled as she offered a prayer of thanks to God.

Printed in the United States
by Baker & Taylor Publisher Services